Disney Princess

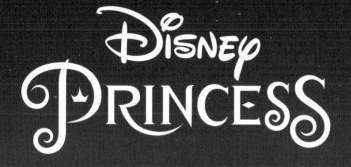

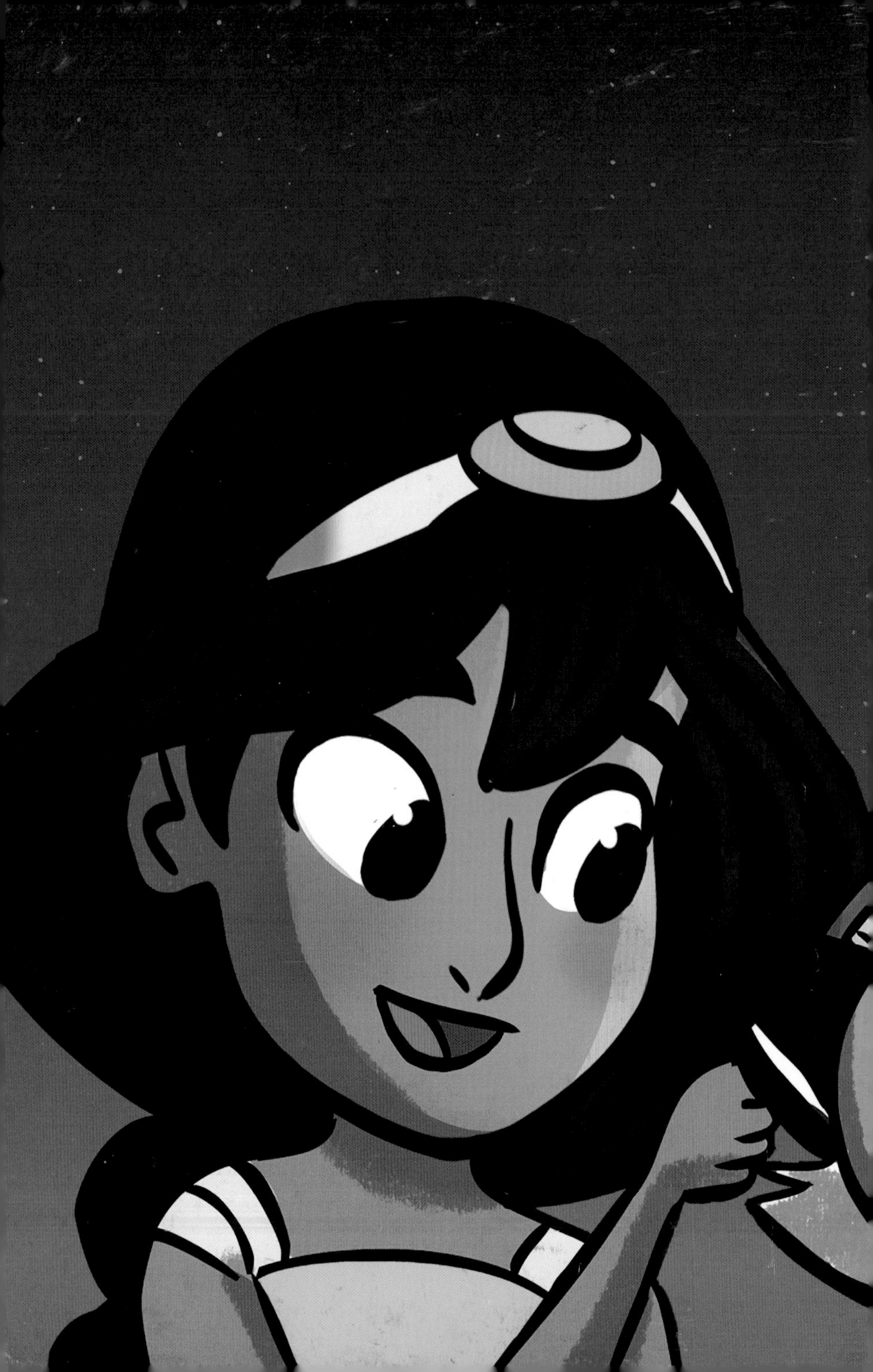

# Disney Princess

## Jasmine's New Pet

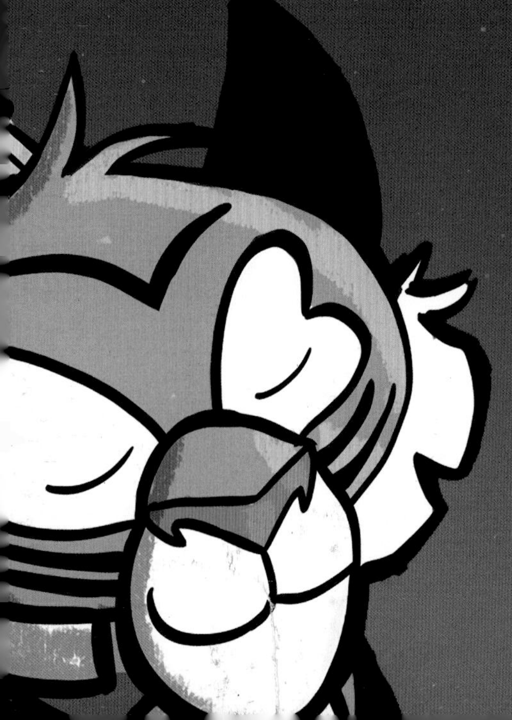

Script and Art by
NIDHI CHANANI

Lettering by
CHRIS DICKEY

Dark Horse Books

# Princess Jasmine

Princess Jasmine is generous, brave, curious, and free-spirited. She sees the good in others and strives to make a difference in the world.

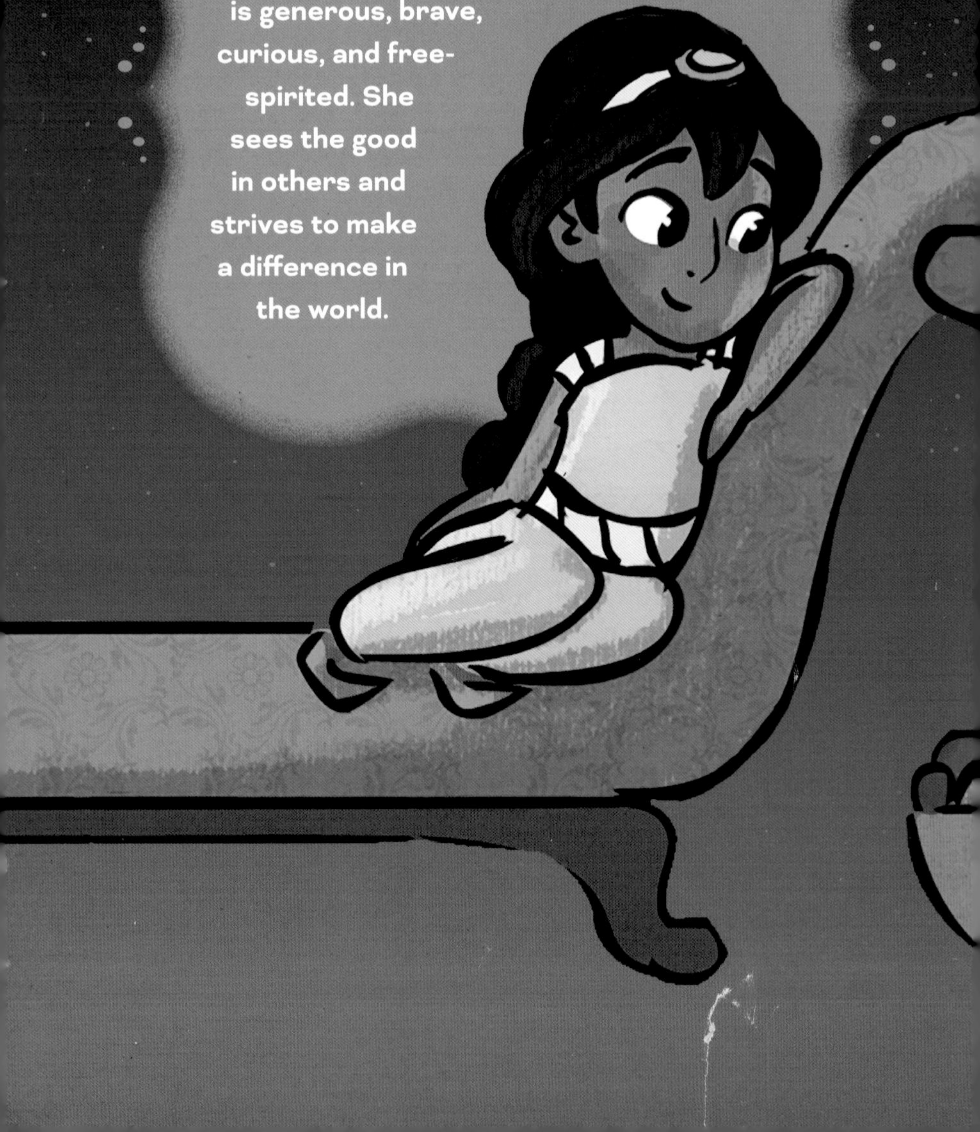

# ⁂ The Sultan ⁂

The Sultan is the father of Princess Jasmine and the ruler of Agrabah. He is sweet, jolly, and gentle. Despite his busy life, he always makes time for his family.

# ⁂ Rajah ⁂

Rajah is a friendly and playful tiger. Still a cub, he loves to run around, get treats, and chase anything that moves.

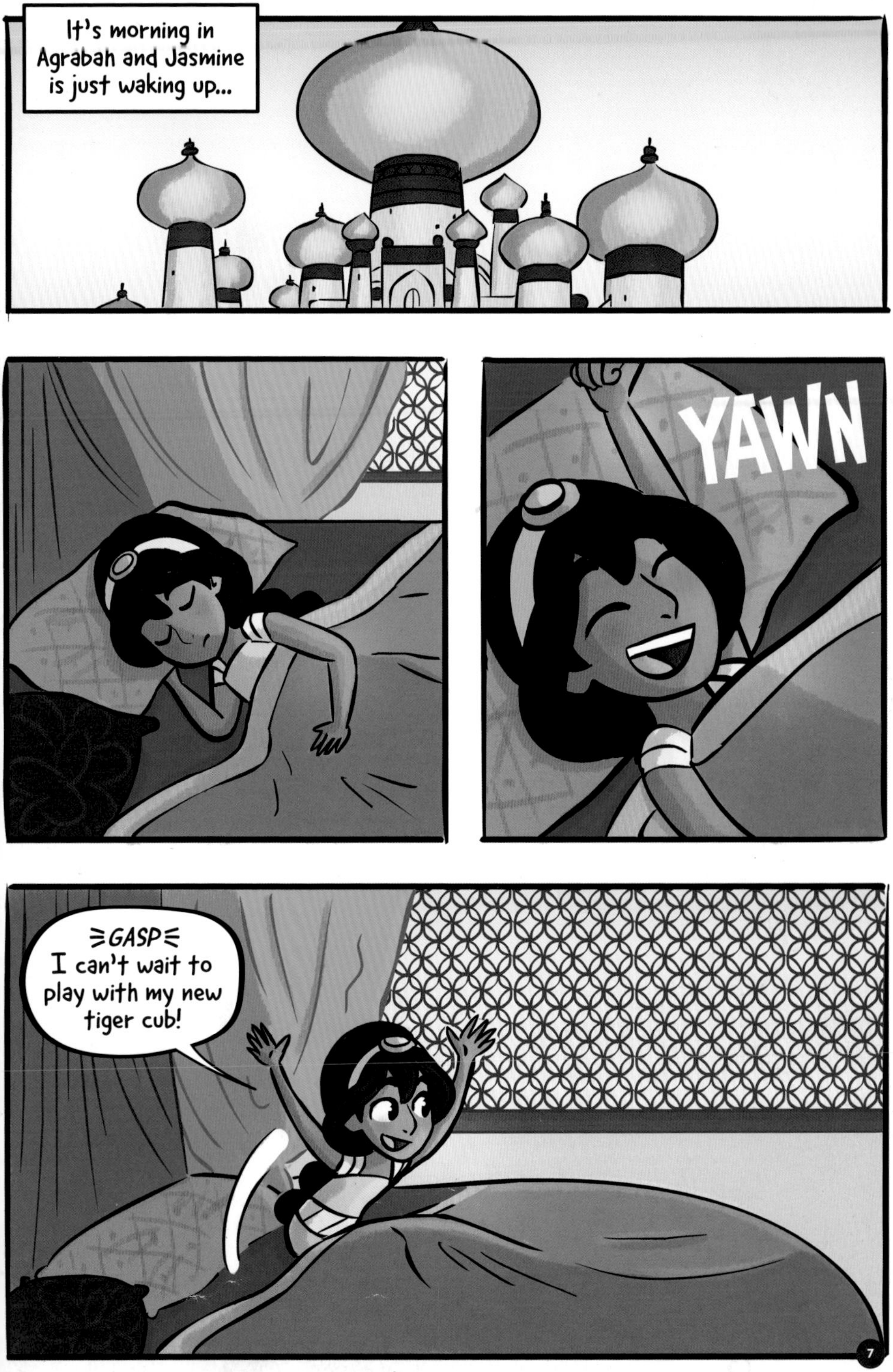
It's morning in Agrabah and Jasmine is just waking up...
YAWN
⋛GASP⋚
I can't wait to play with my new tiger cub!

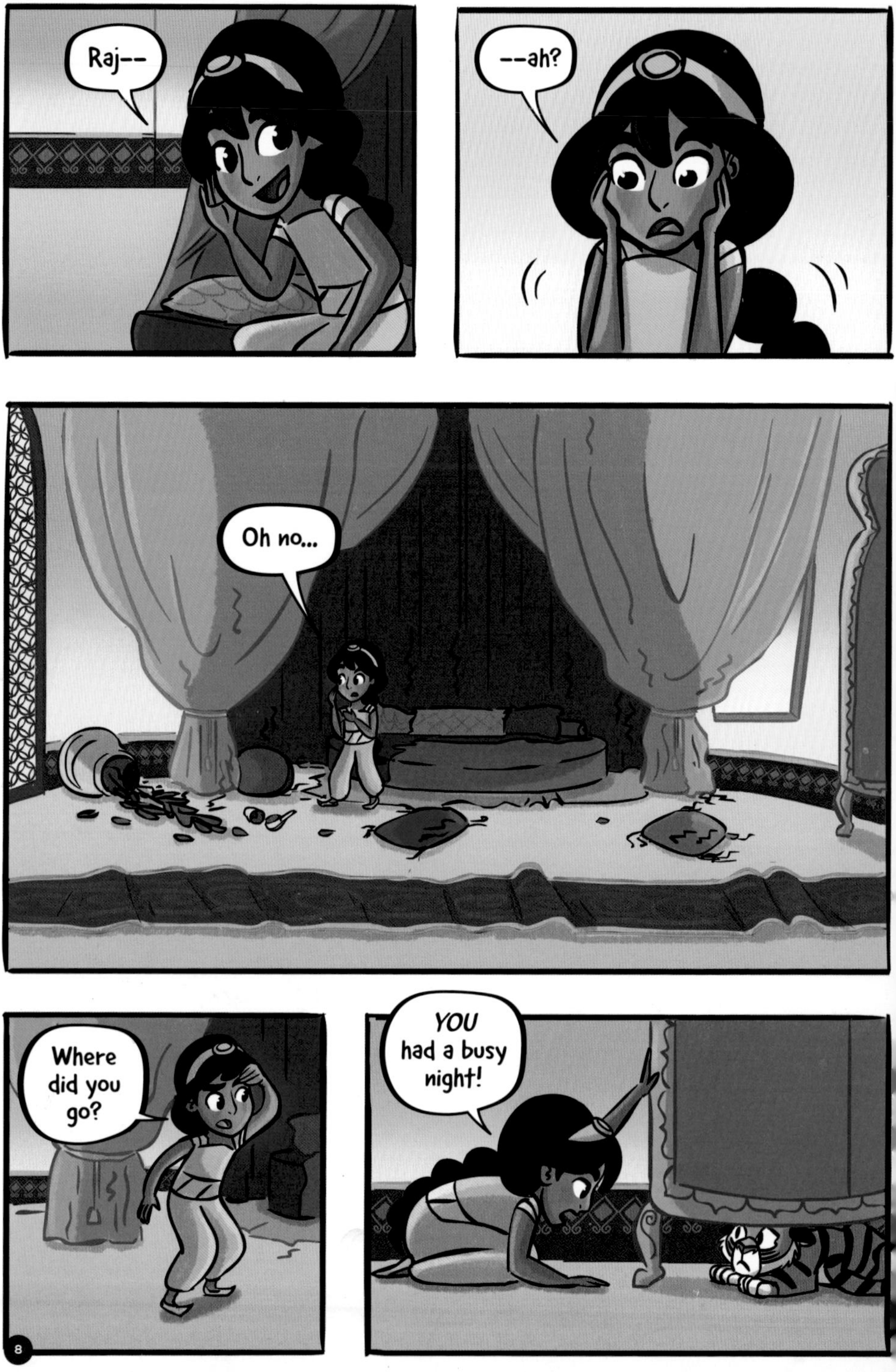
Raj--
--ah?
Oh no...
Where did you go?
*YOU* had a busy night!

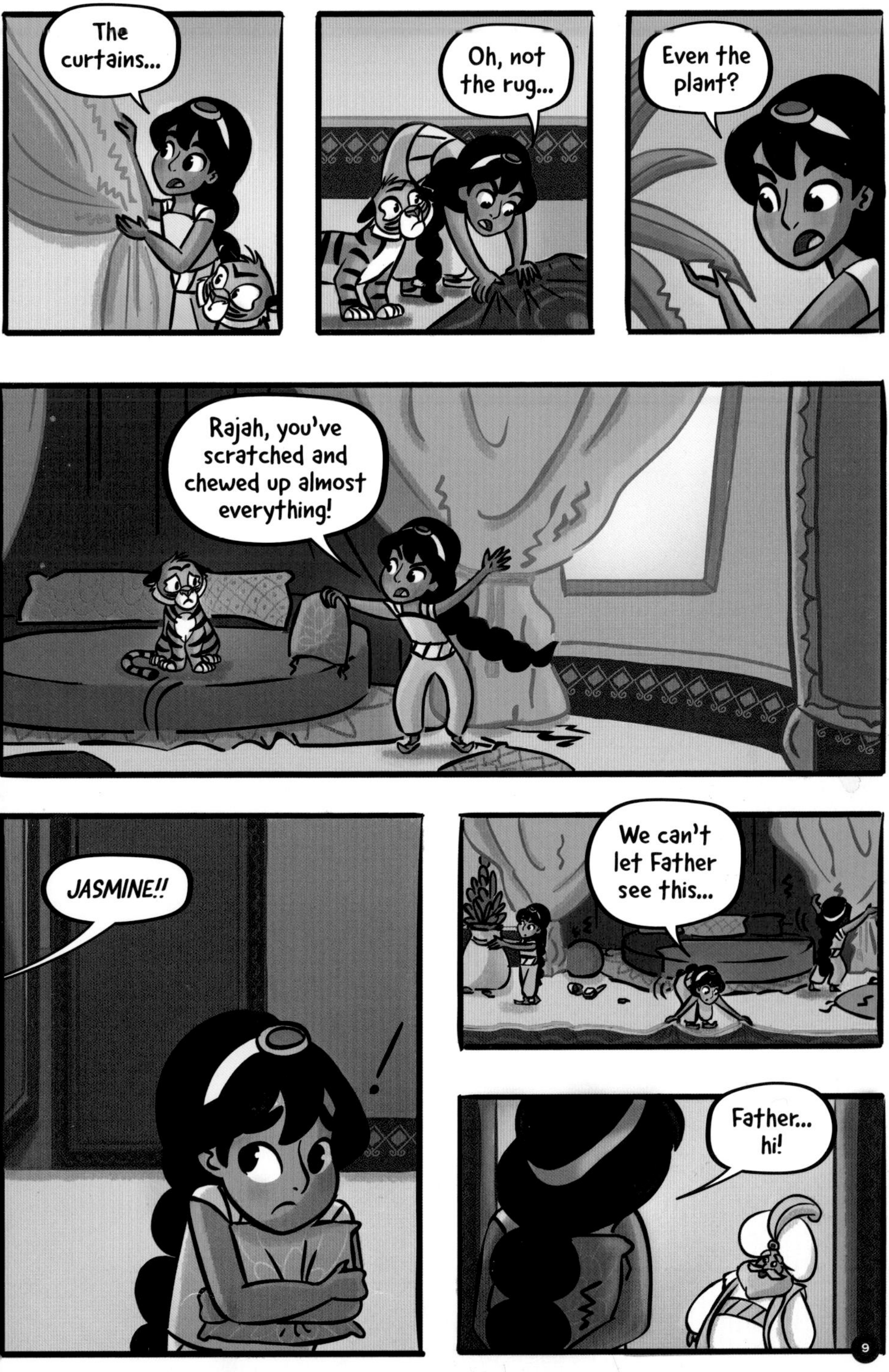
The curtains...
Oh, not the rug...
Even the plant?
Rajah, you've scratched and chewed up almost everything!
JASMINE!!
We can't let Father see this...
Father... hi!

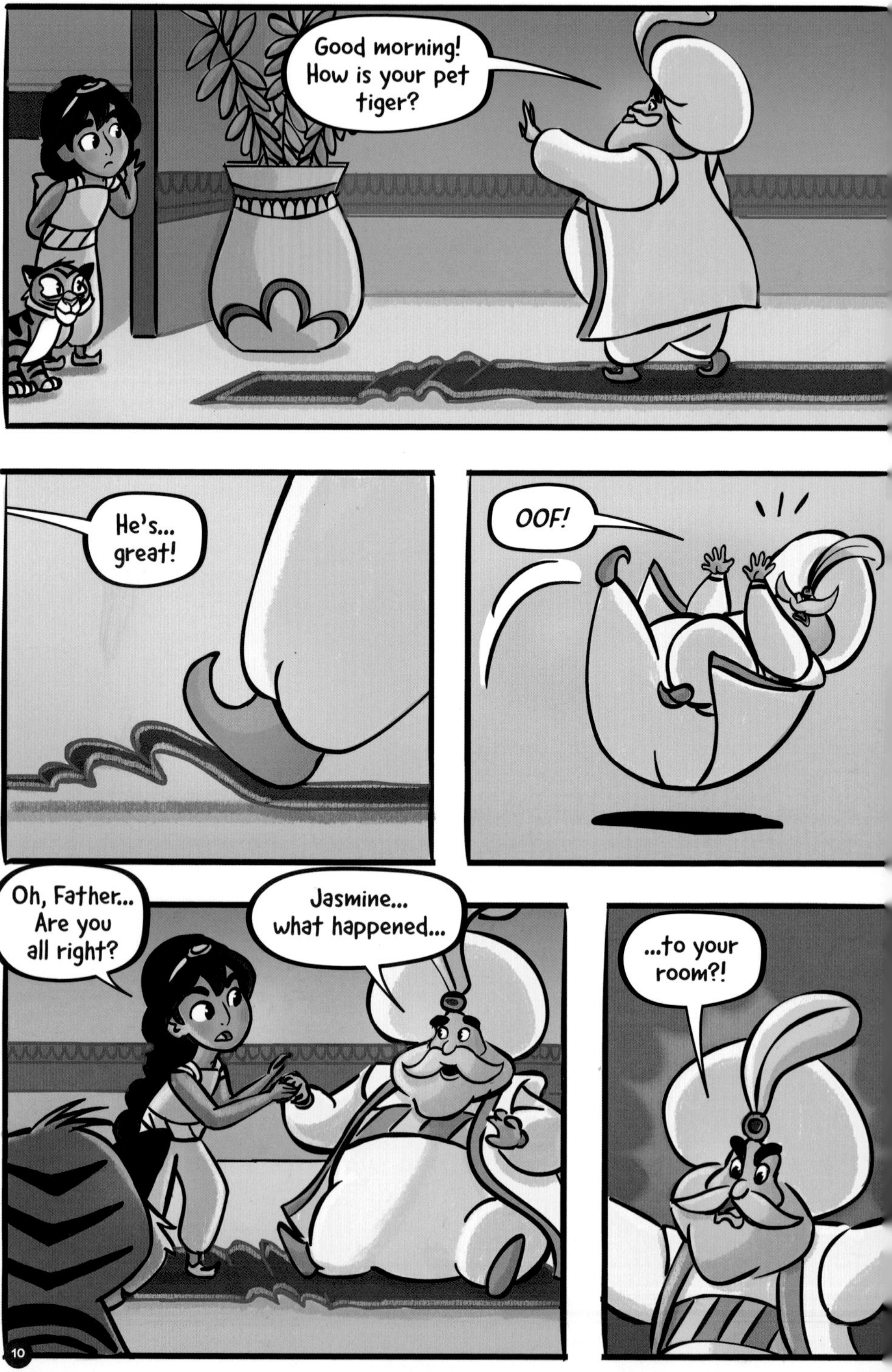

Good morning! How is your pet tiger?
He's... great!
OOF!
Oh, Father... Are you all right?
Jasmine... what happened...
...to your room?!

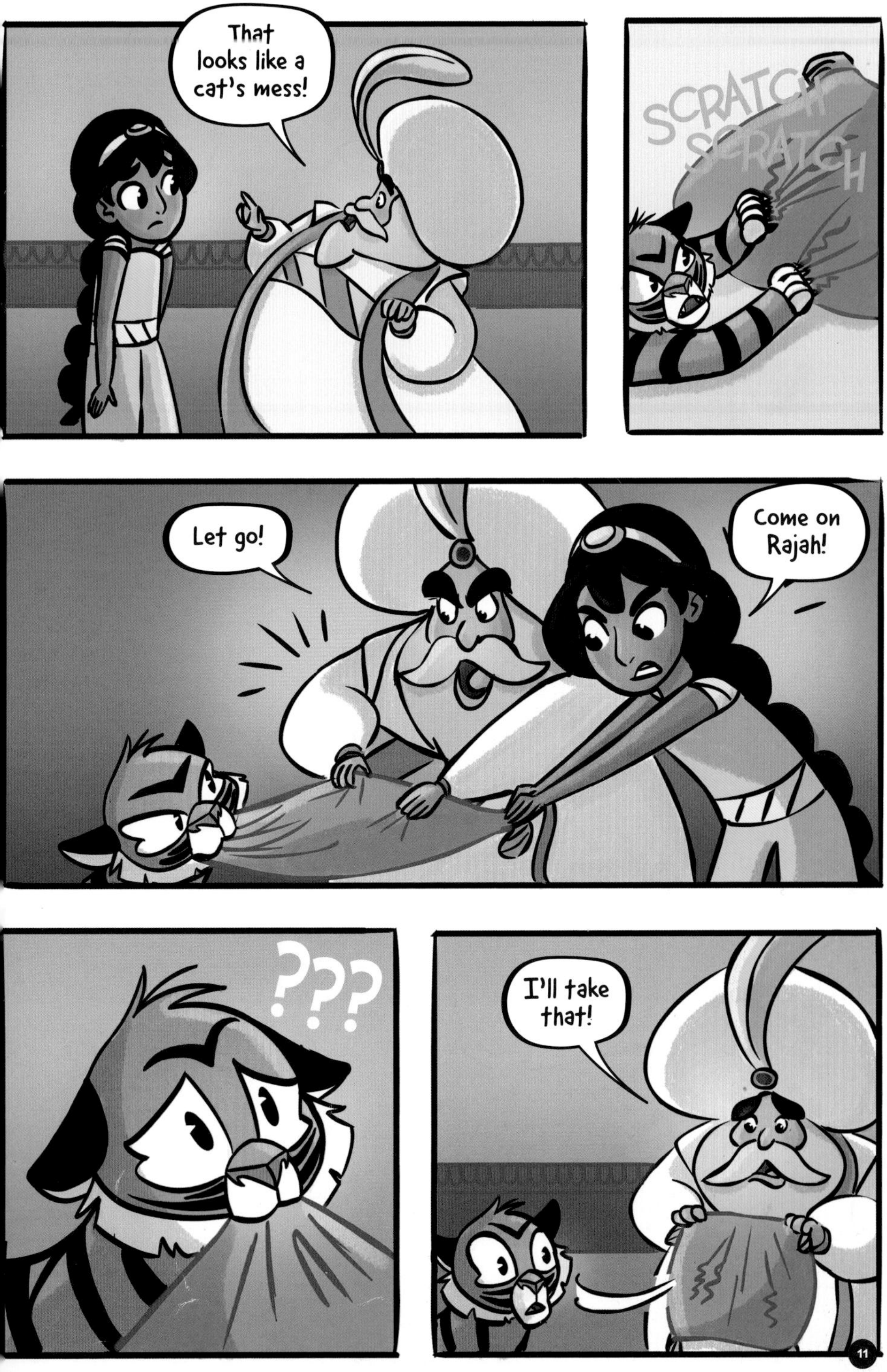

That looks like a cat's mess!
SCRATCH SCRATCH
Let go!
Come on Rajah!
???
I'll take that!

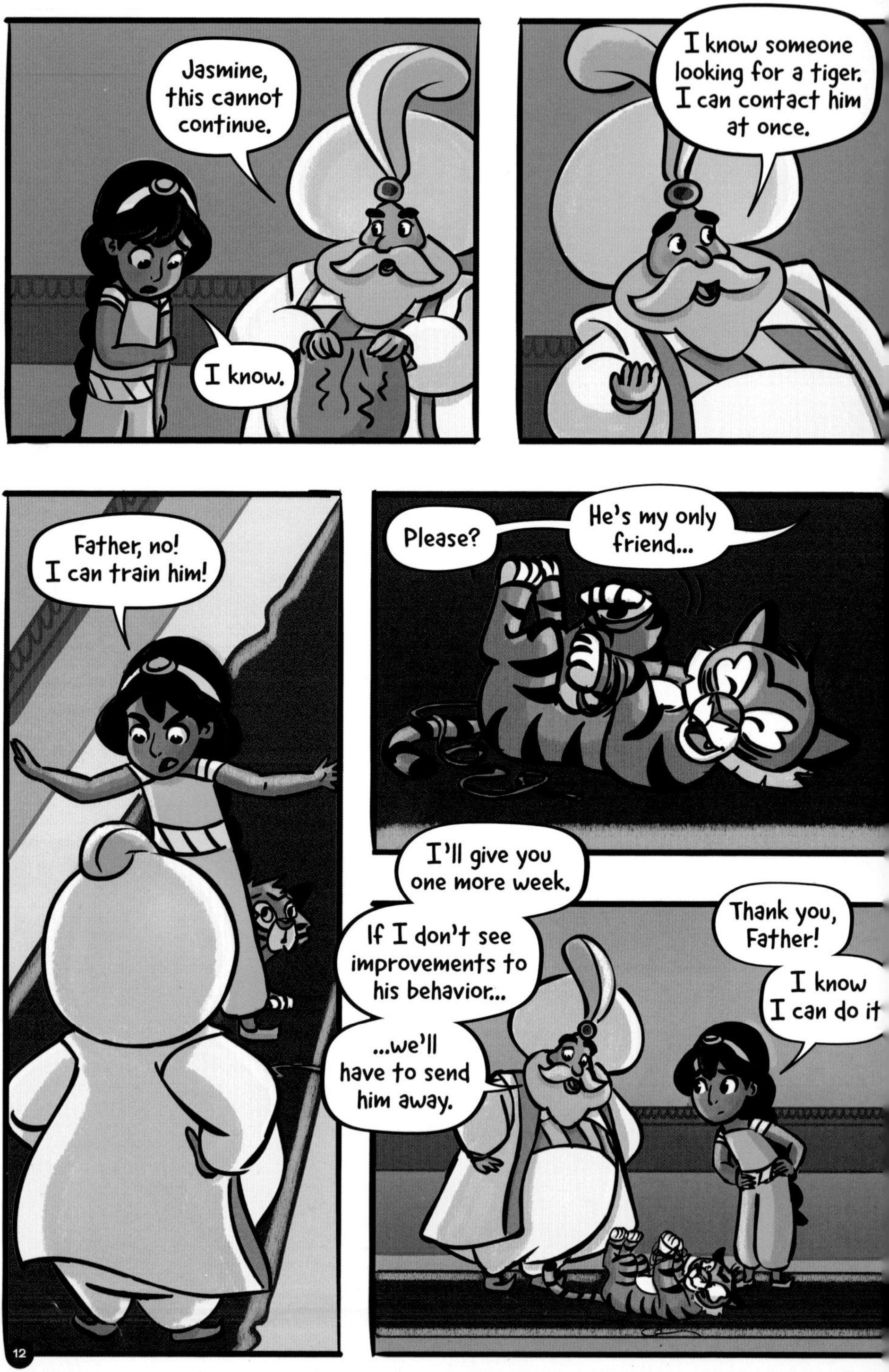
Jasmine, this cannot continue.
I know.
I know someone looking for a tiger. I can contact him at once.
Father, no! I can train him!
Please?
He's my only friend...
I'll give you one more week.
If I don't see improvements to his behavior...
...we'll have to send him away.
Thank you, Father!
I know I can do it

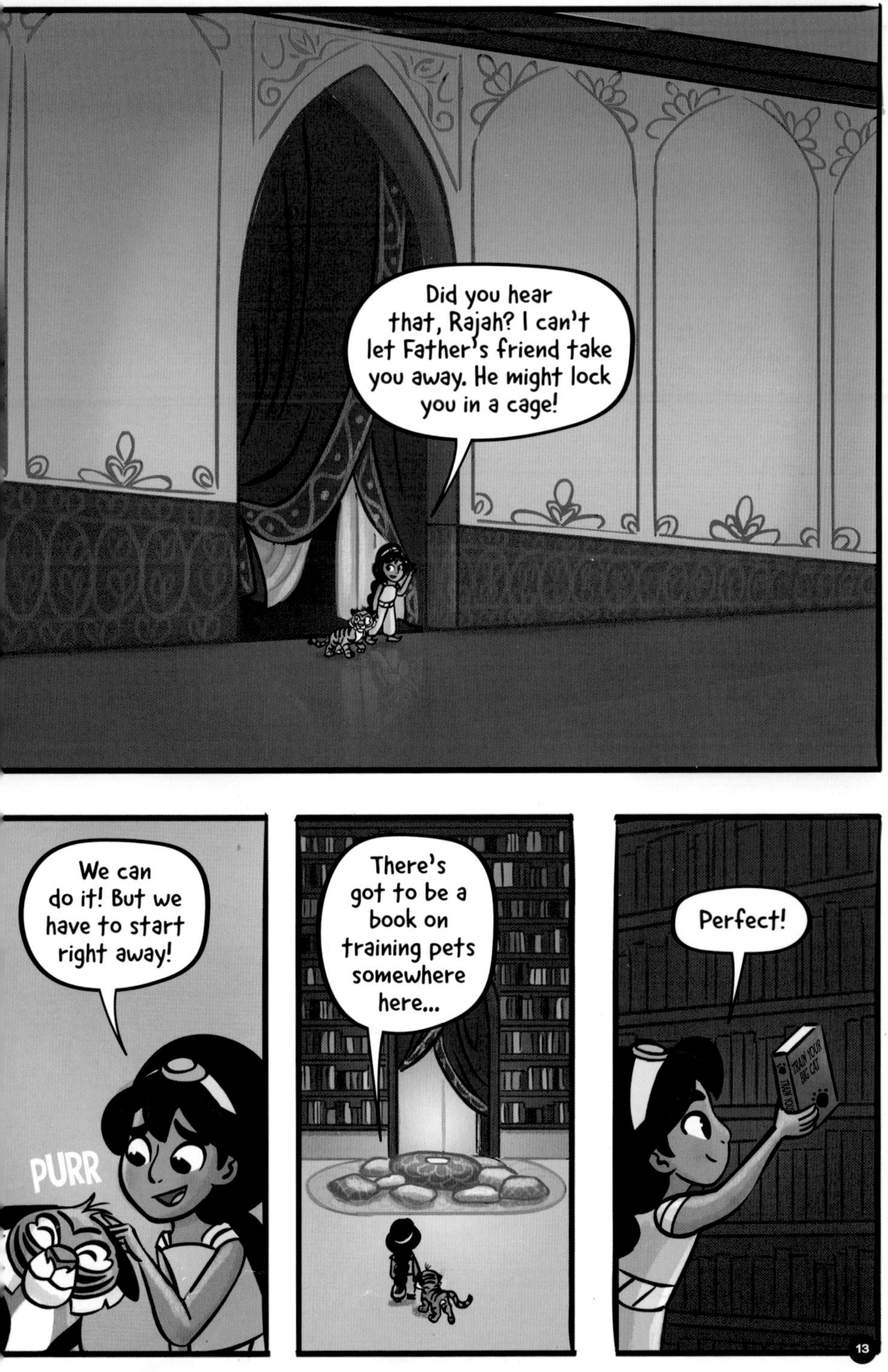
Did you hear that, Rajah? I can't let Father's friend take you away. He might lock you in a cage!
We can do it! But we have to start right away!
PURR
There's got to be a book on training pets somewhere here...
Perfect!
TRAIN YOUR BIG CAT

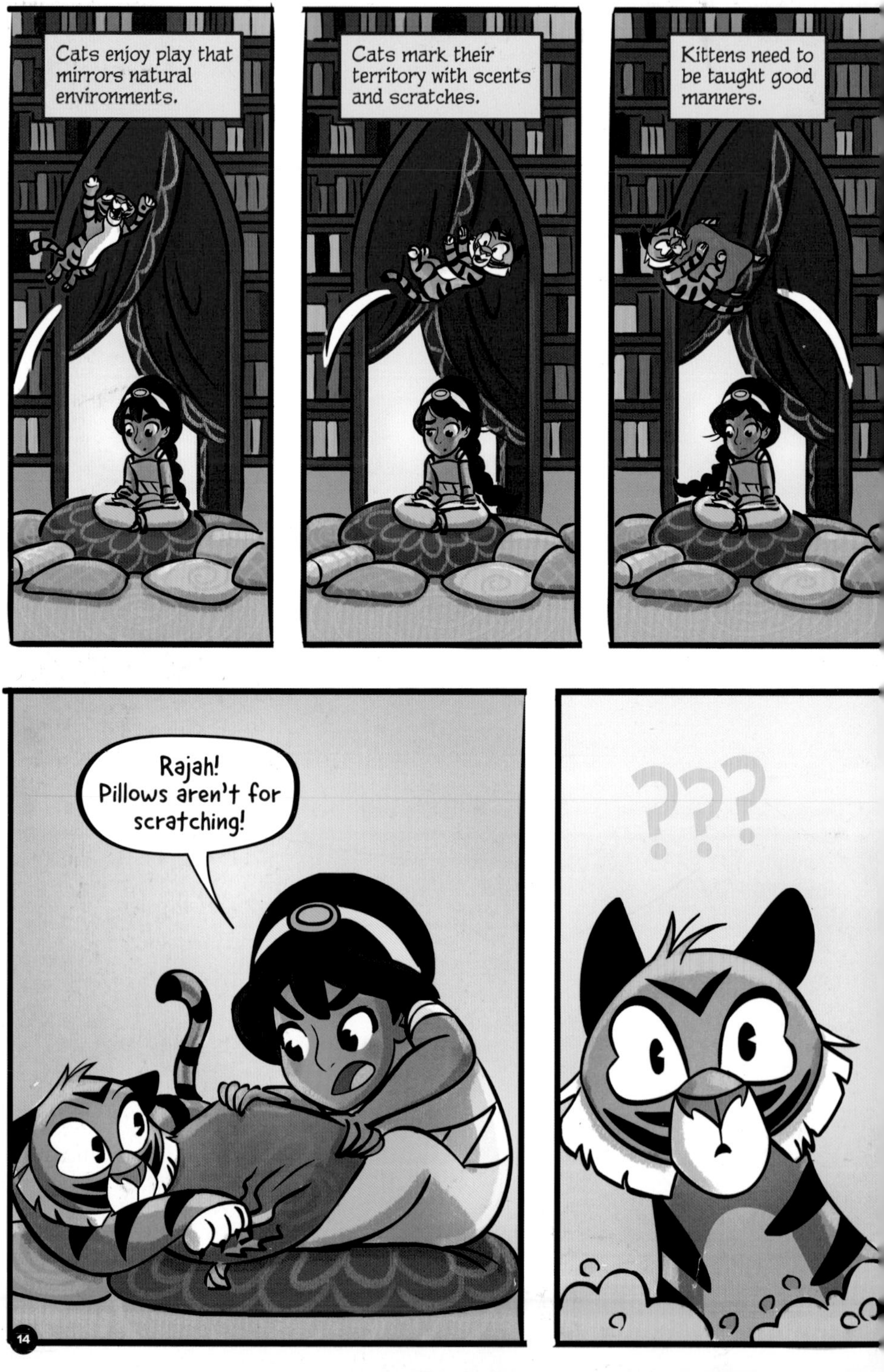
Cats enjoy play that mirrors natural environments.
Cats mark their territory with scents and scratches.
Kittens need to be taught good manners.
Rajah! Pillows aren't for scratching!
???

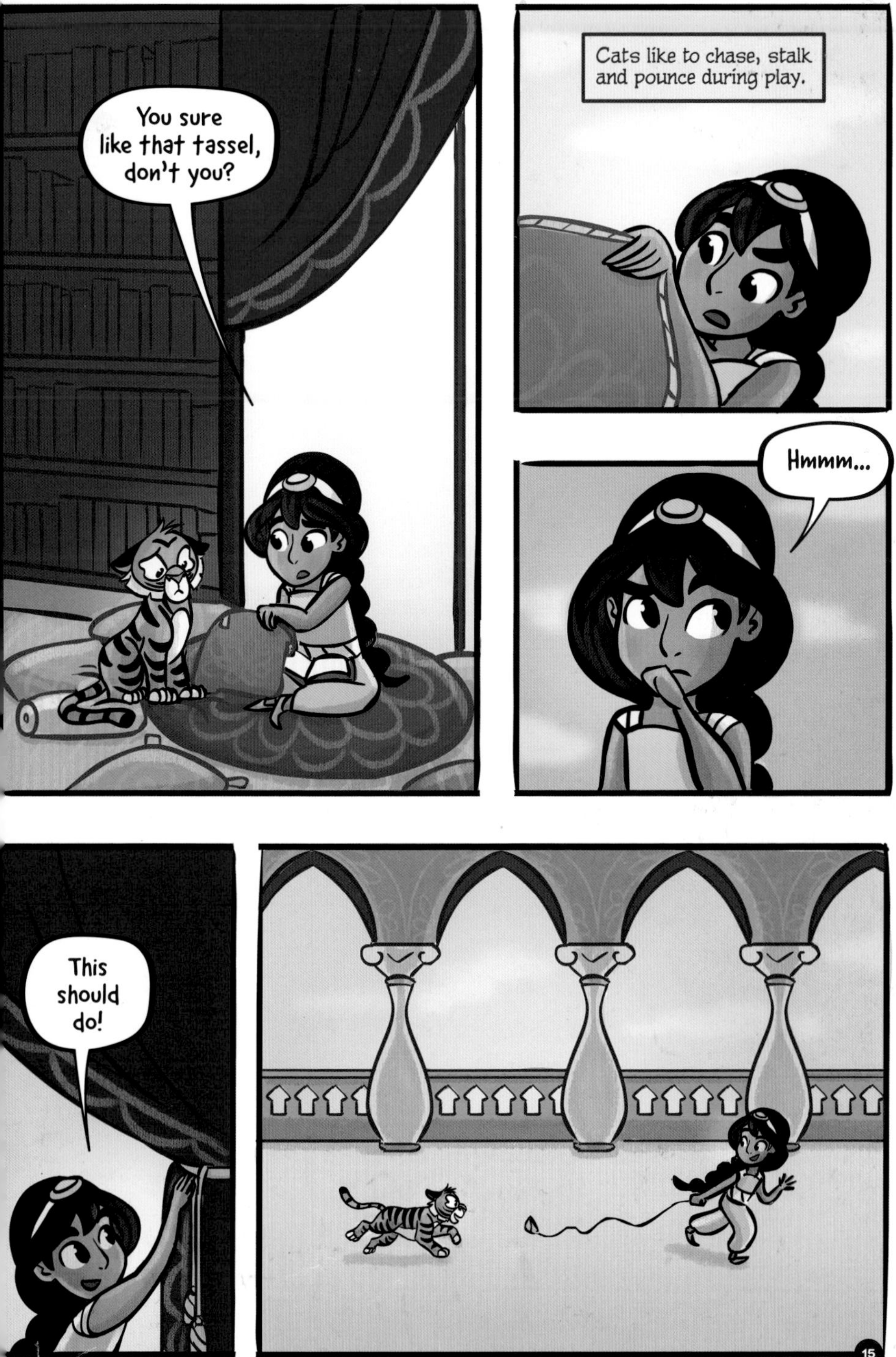
You sure like that tassel, don't you?
Cats like to chase, stalk and pounce during play.
Hmmm...
This should do!

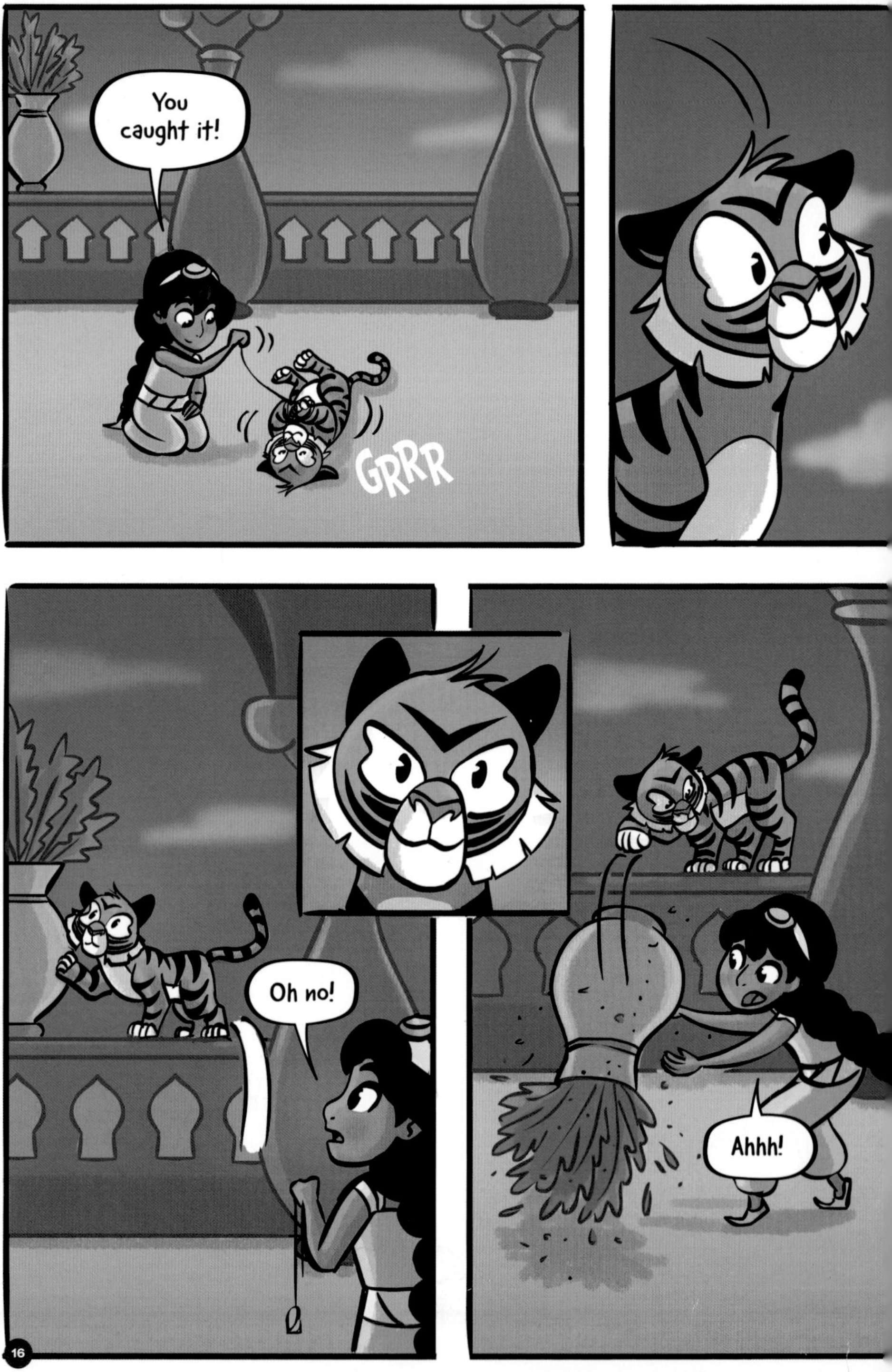
You caught it!
GRRR
Oh no!
Ahhh!

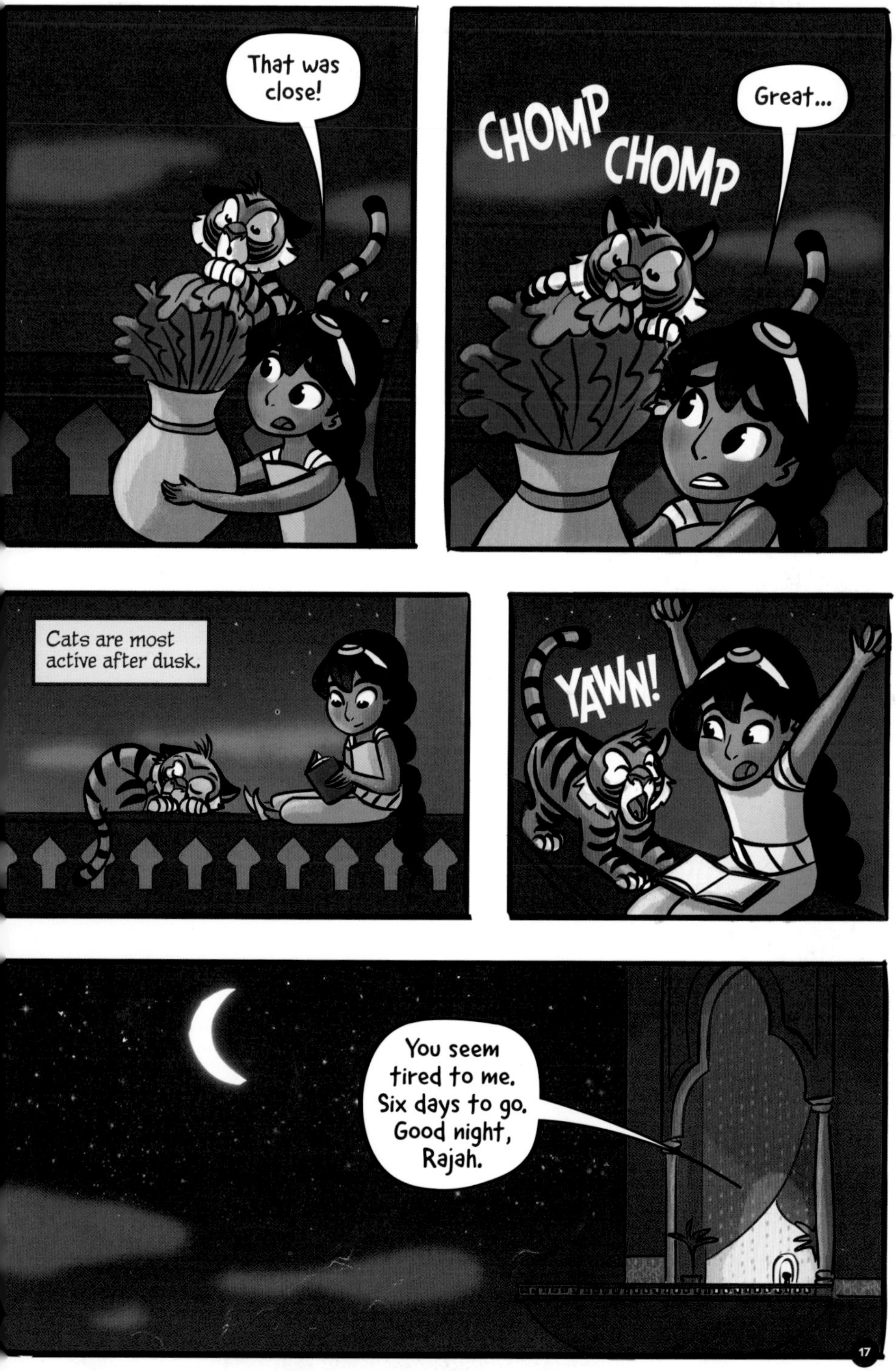
That was close!
CHOMP CHOMP
Great...
Cats are most active after dusk.
YAWN!
You seem tired to me. Six days to go. Good night, Rajah.

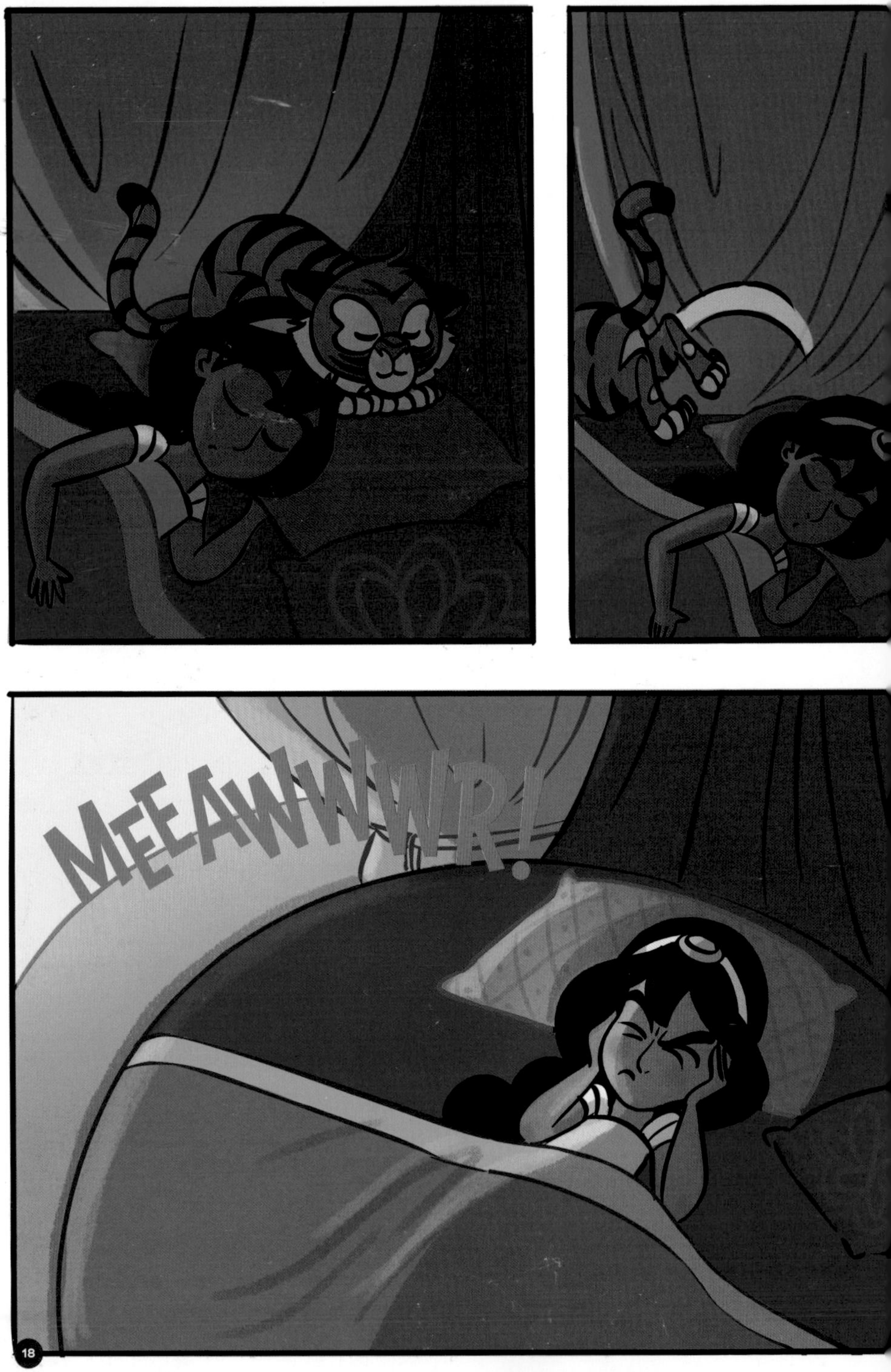
MEEAWWWR!

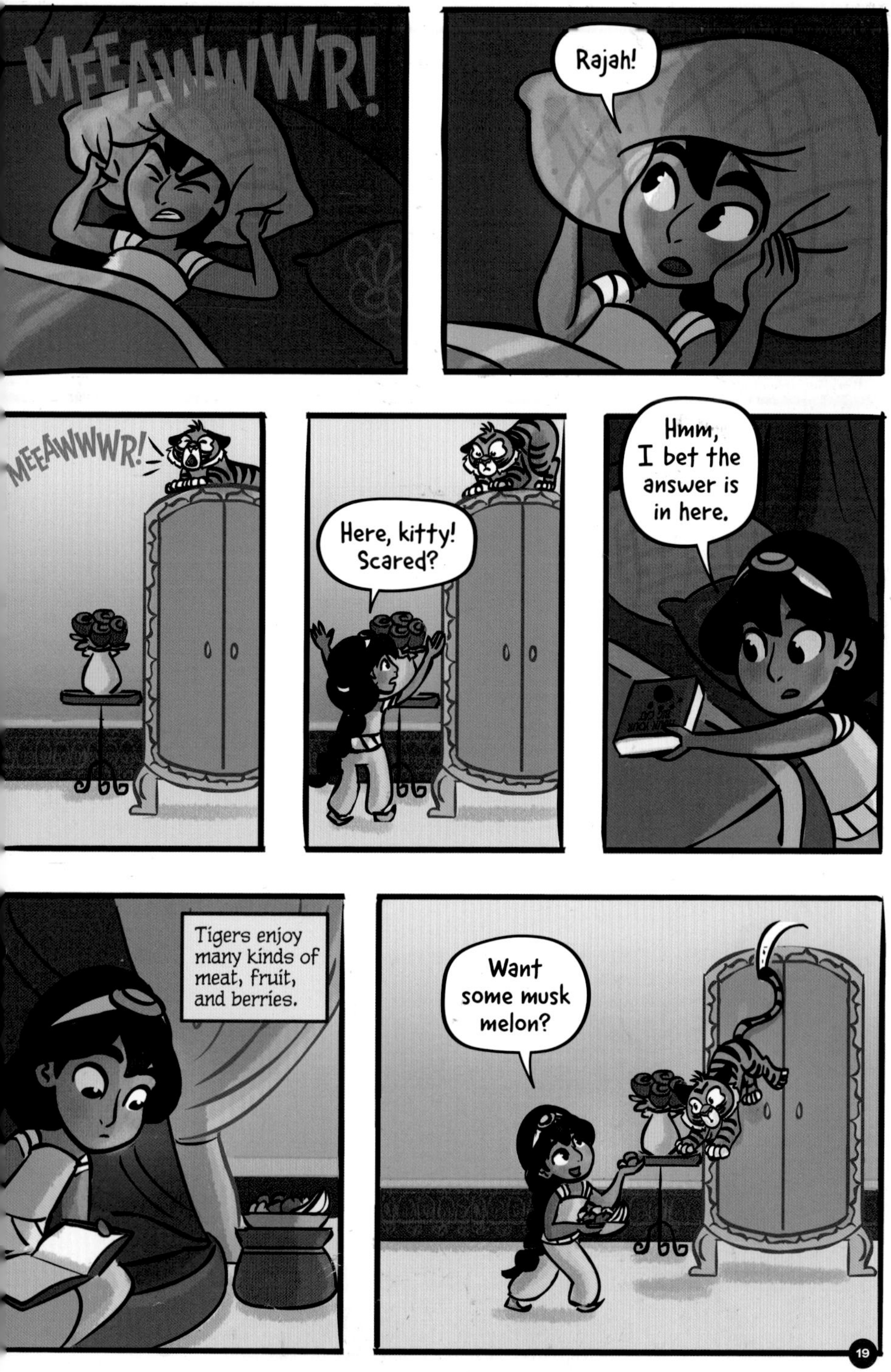
MEEAWWWR!
Rajah!
MEEAWWWR!
Here, kitty! Scared?
Hmm, I bet the answer is in here.
Tigers enjoy many kinds of meat, fruit, and berries.
Want some musk melon?

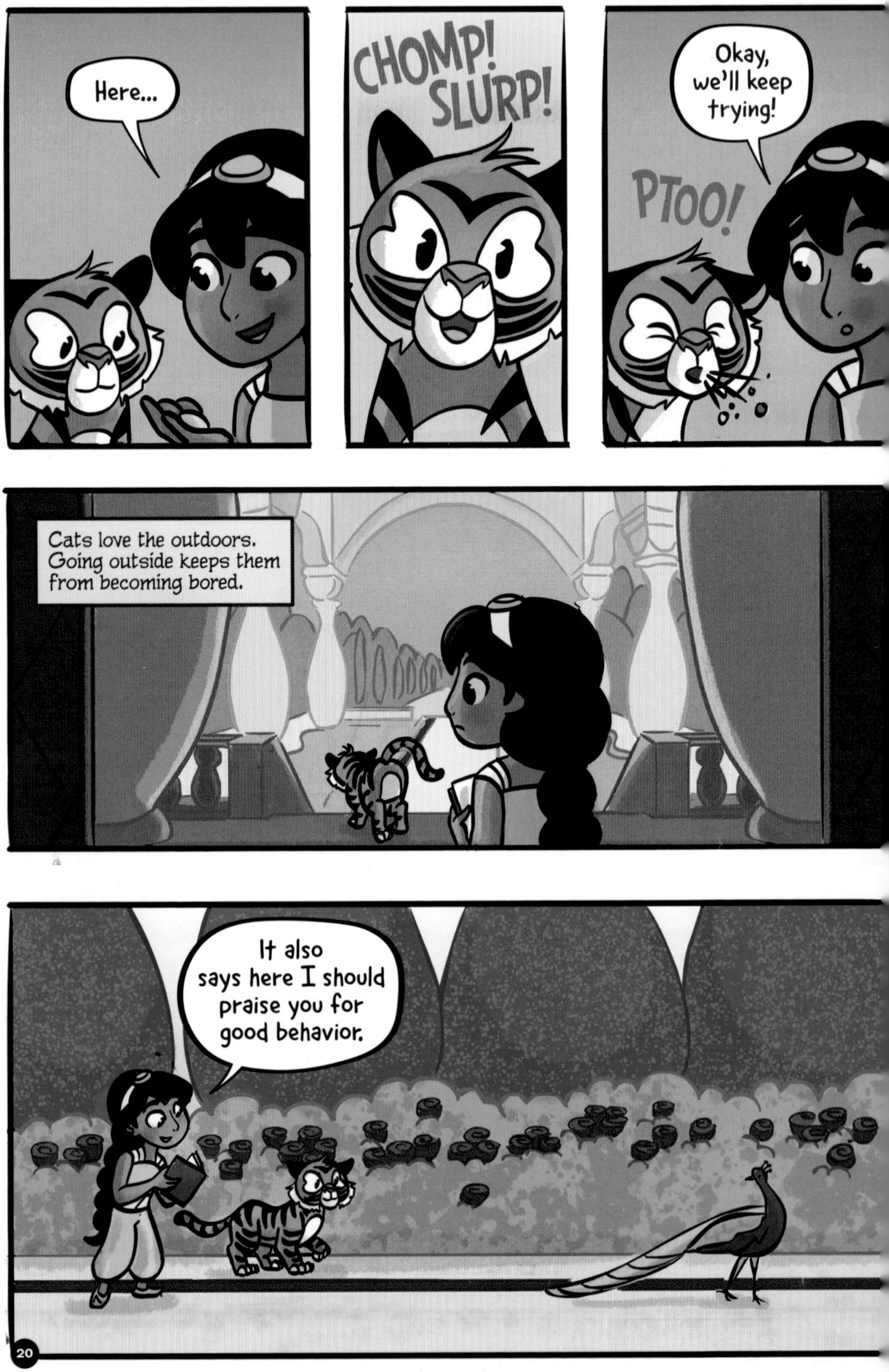
Here...
CHOMP! SLURP!
Okay, we'll keep trying!
PTOO!
Cats love the outdoors. Going outside keeps them from becoming bored.
It also says here I should praise you for good behavior.

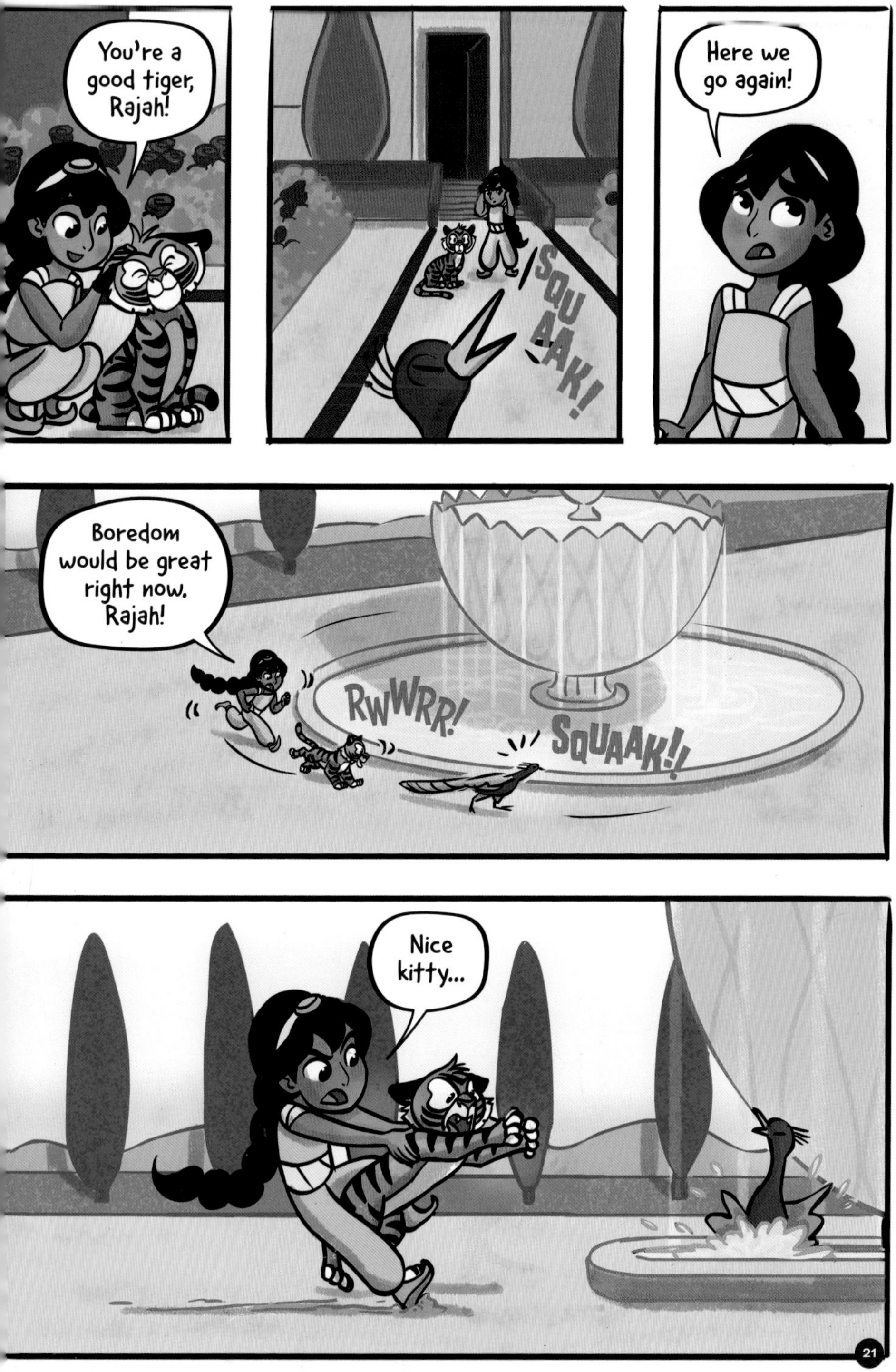
You're a good tiger, Rajah!
SQUAAAK!
Here we go again!
Boredom would be great right now. Rajah!
RWWRR!
SQUAAK!!
Nice kitty...

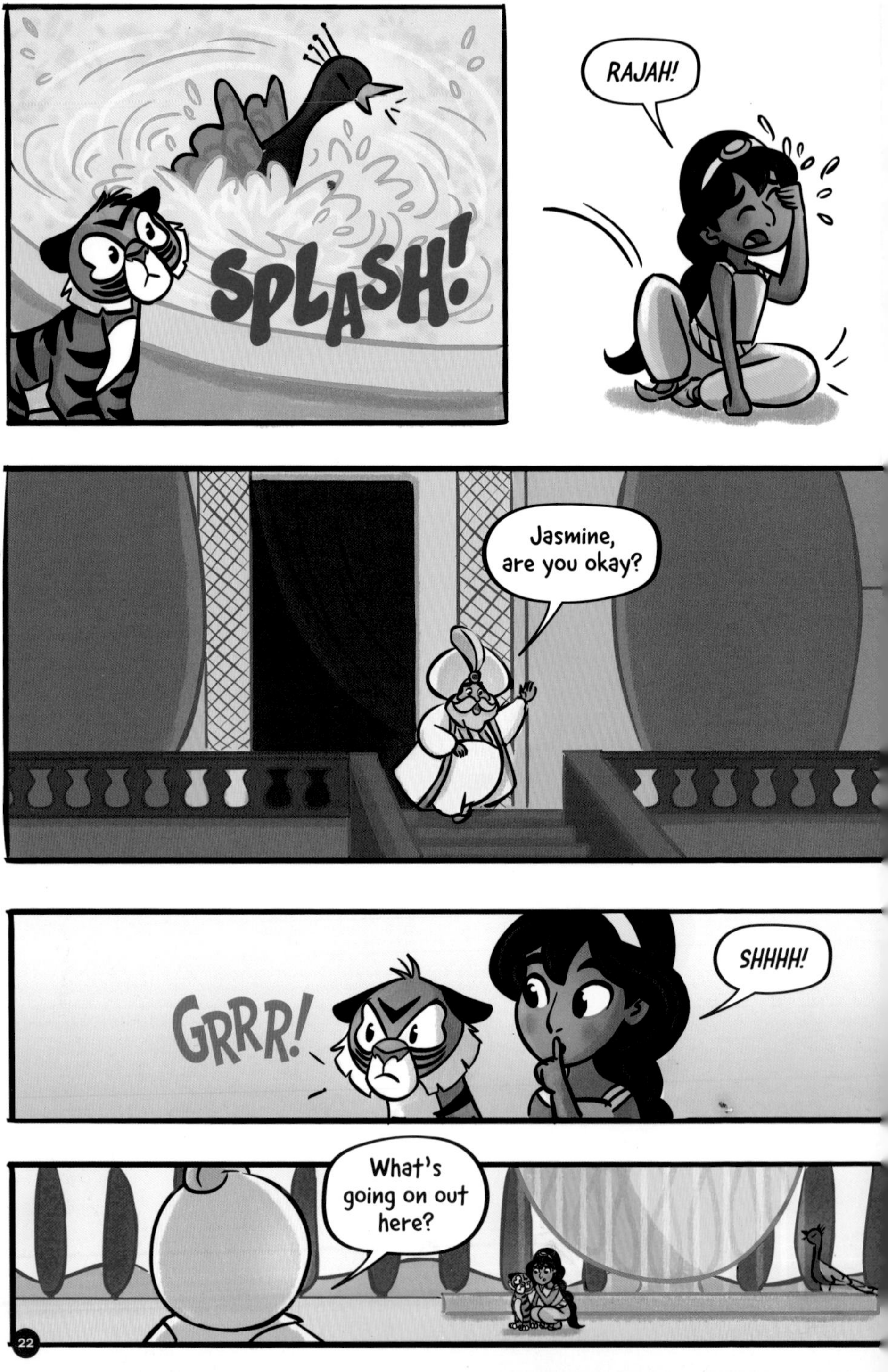
SPLASH!
RAJAH!
Jasmine, are you okay?
GRRR!
SHHHH!
What's going on out here?

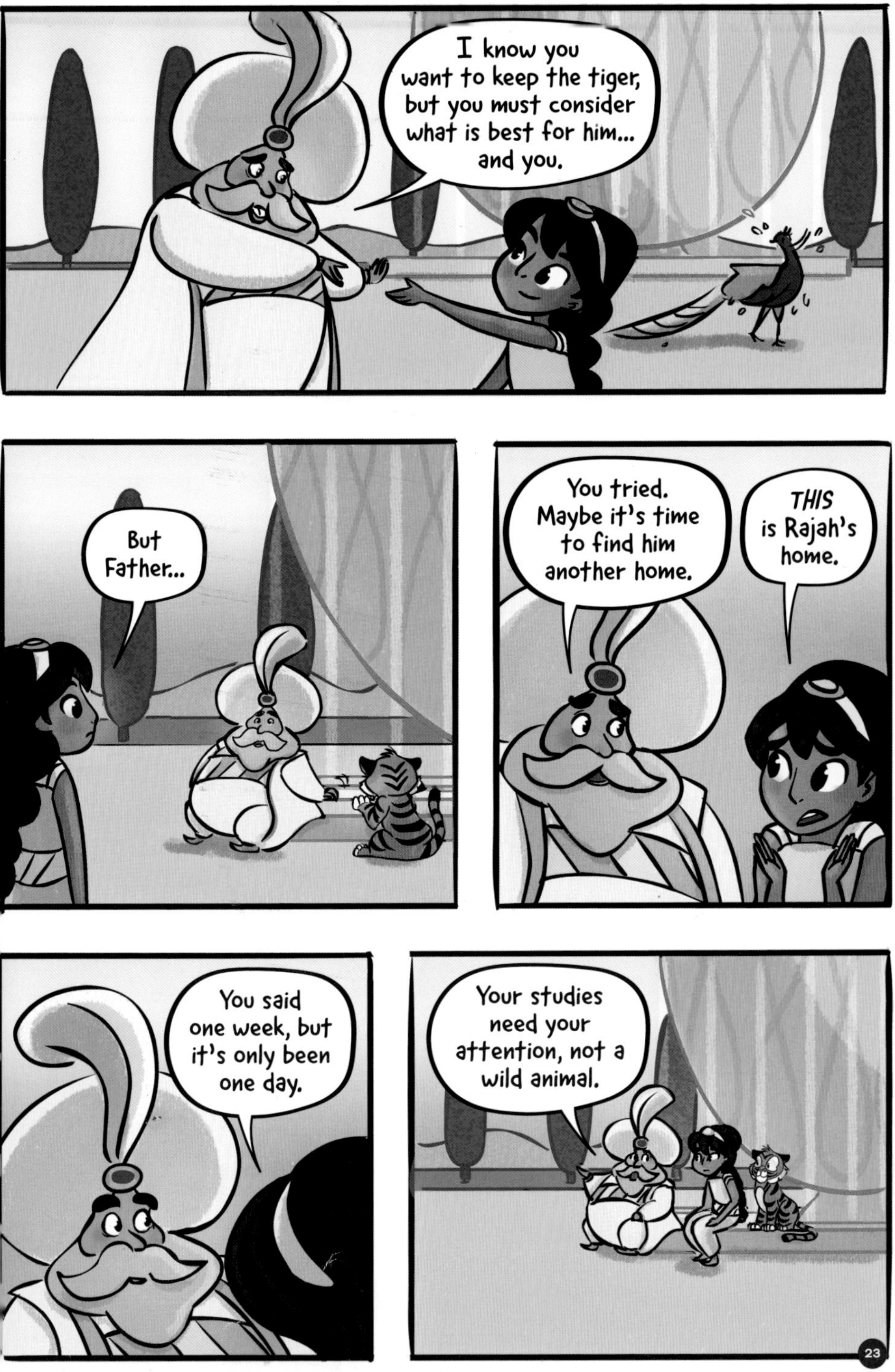
I know you want to keep the tiger, but you must consider what is best for him... and you.
But Father...
You tried. Maybe it's time to find him another home.
THIS is Rajah's home.
You said one week, but it's only been one day.
Your studies need your attention, not a wild animal.

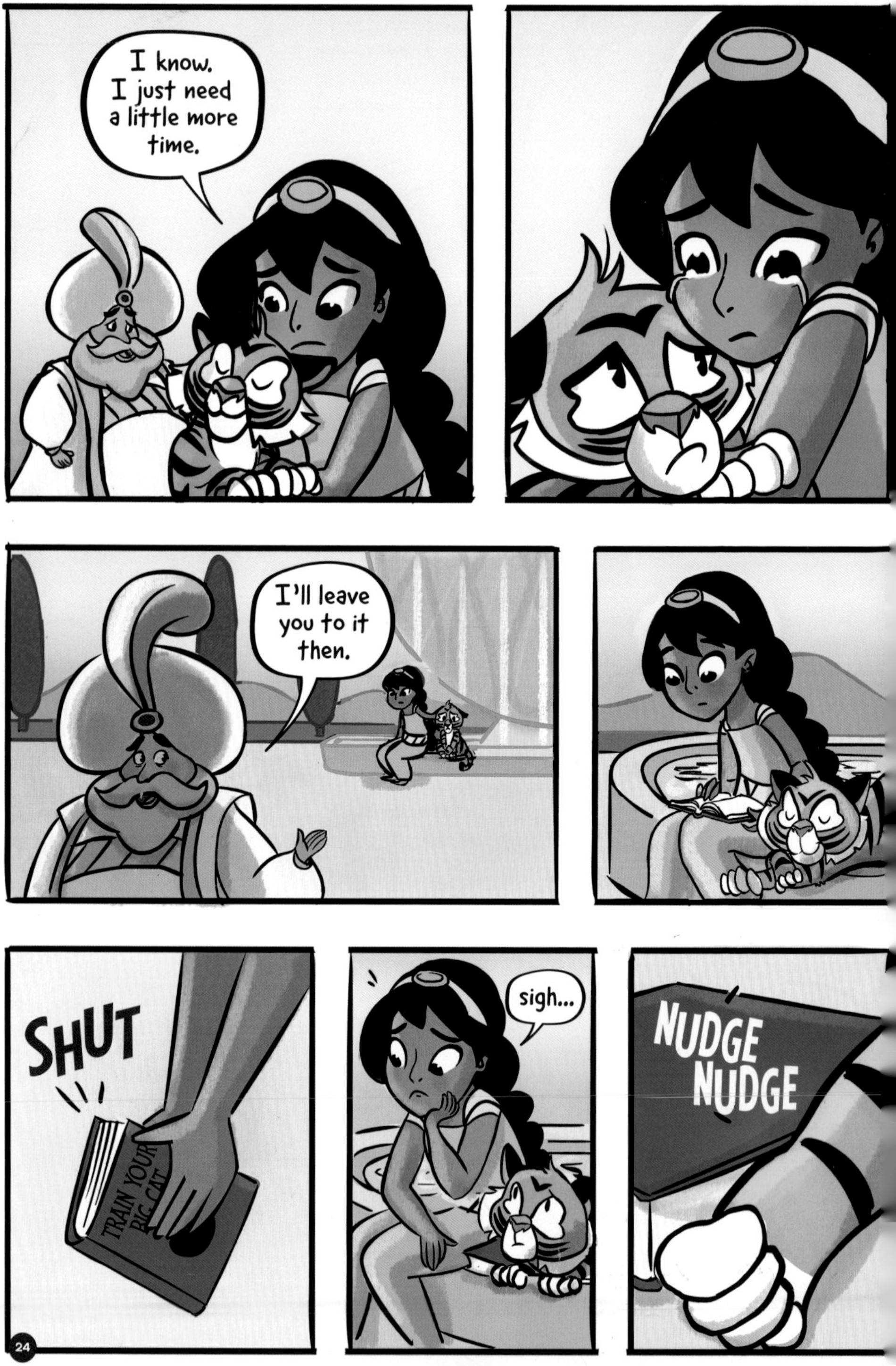
I know. I just need a little more time.
I'll leave you to it then.
SHUT
TRAIN YOUR BIG CAT
sigh...
NUDGE NUDGE

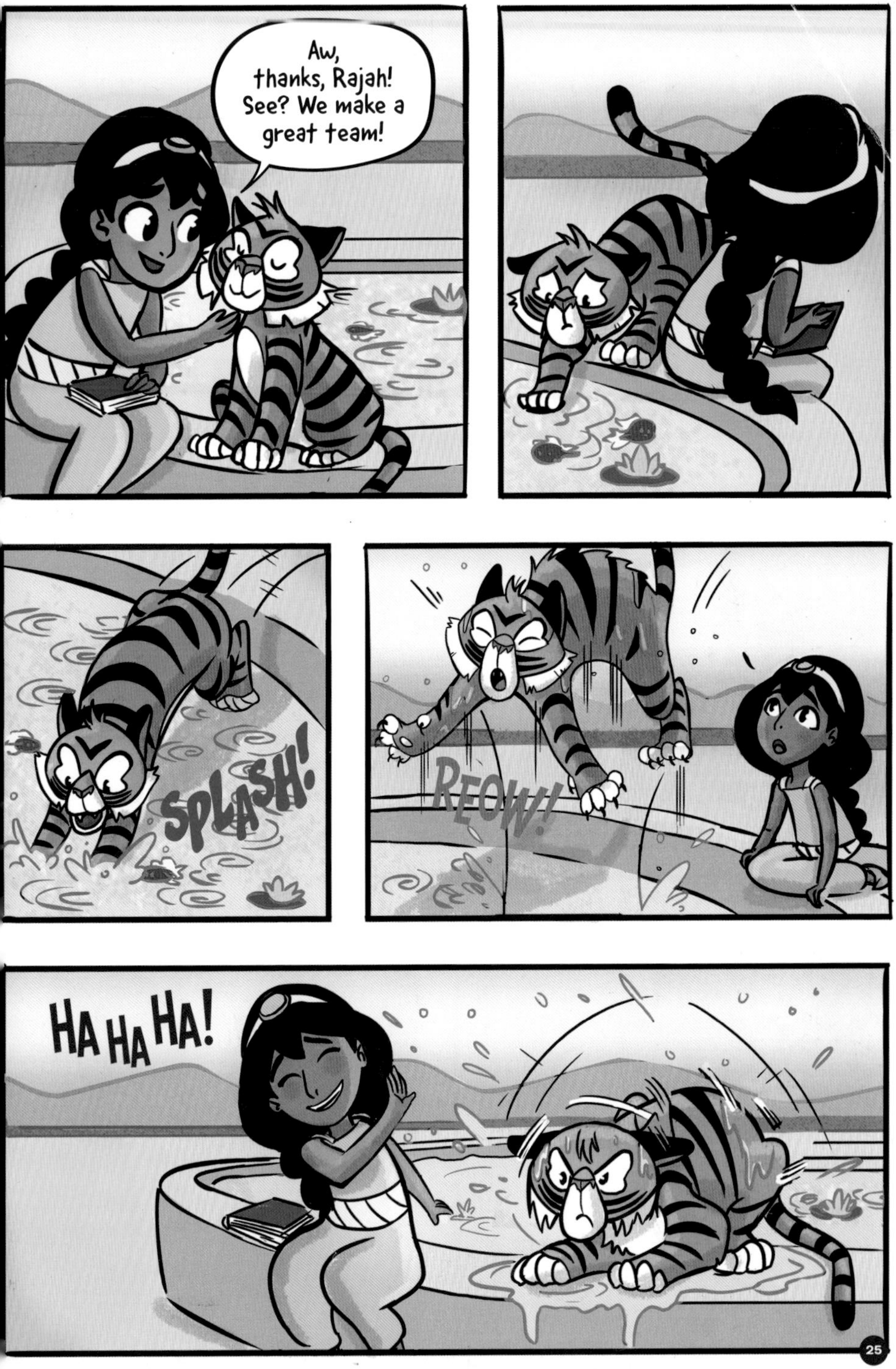
Aw, thanks, Rajah! See? We make a great team!
SPLASH!
REOW!
HA HA HA!

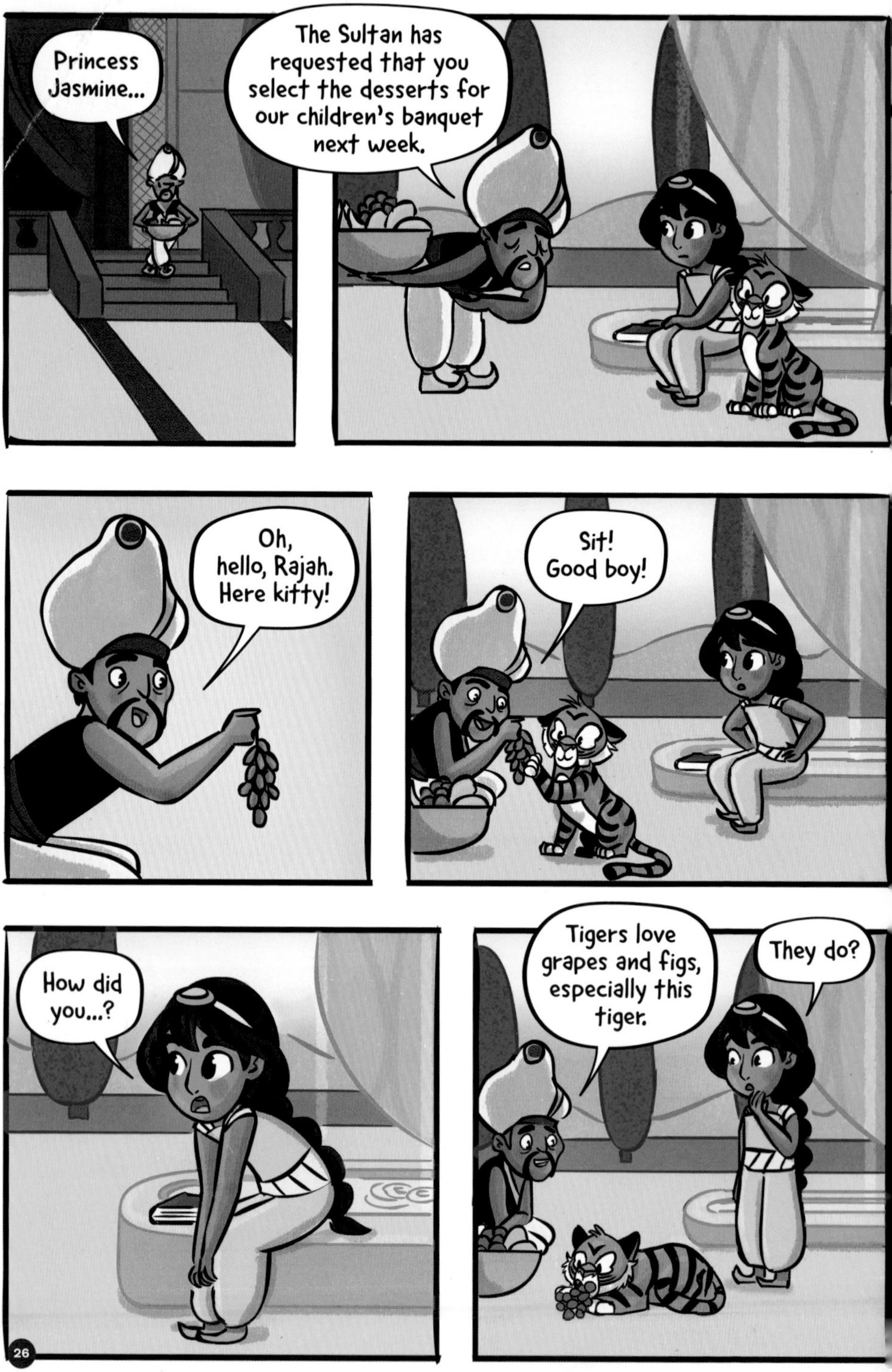
Princess Jasmine...
The Sultan has requested that you select the desserts for our children's banquet next week.
Oh, hello, Rajah. Here kitty!
Sit! Good boy!
How did you...?
Tigers love grapes and figs, especially this tiger.
They do?

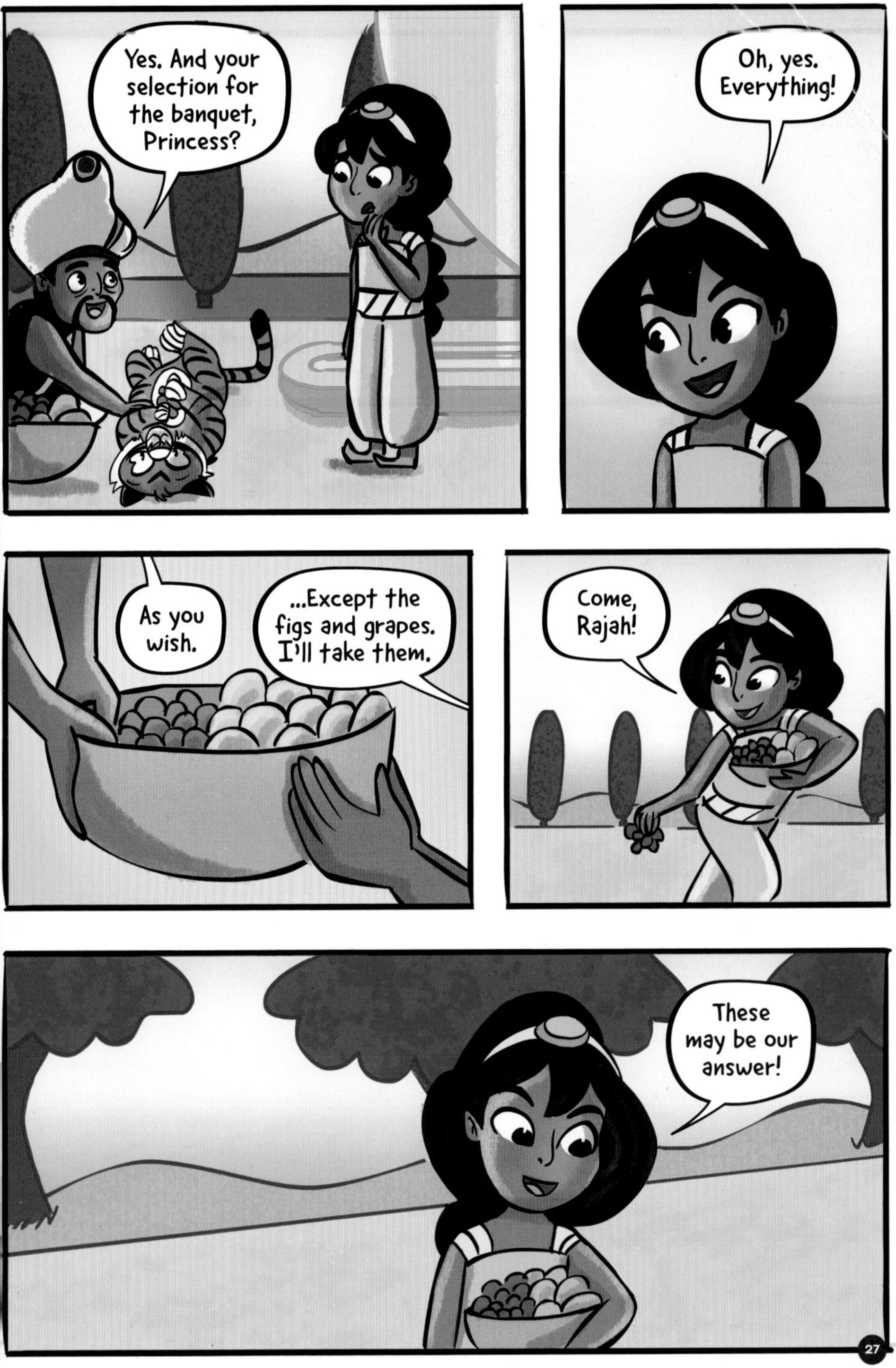
Yes. And your selection for the banquet, Princess?
Oh, yes. Everything!
As you wish.
...Except the figs and grapes. I'll take them.
Come, Rajah!
These may be our answer!

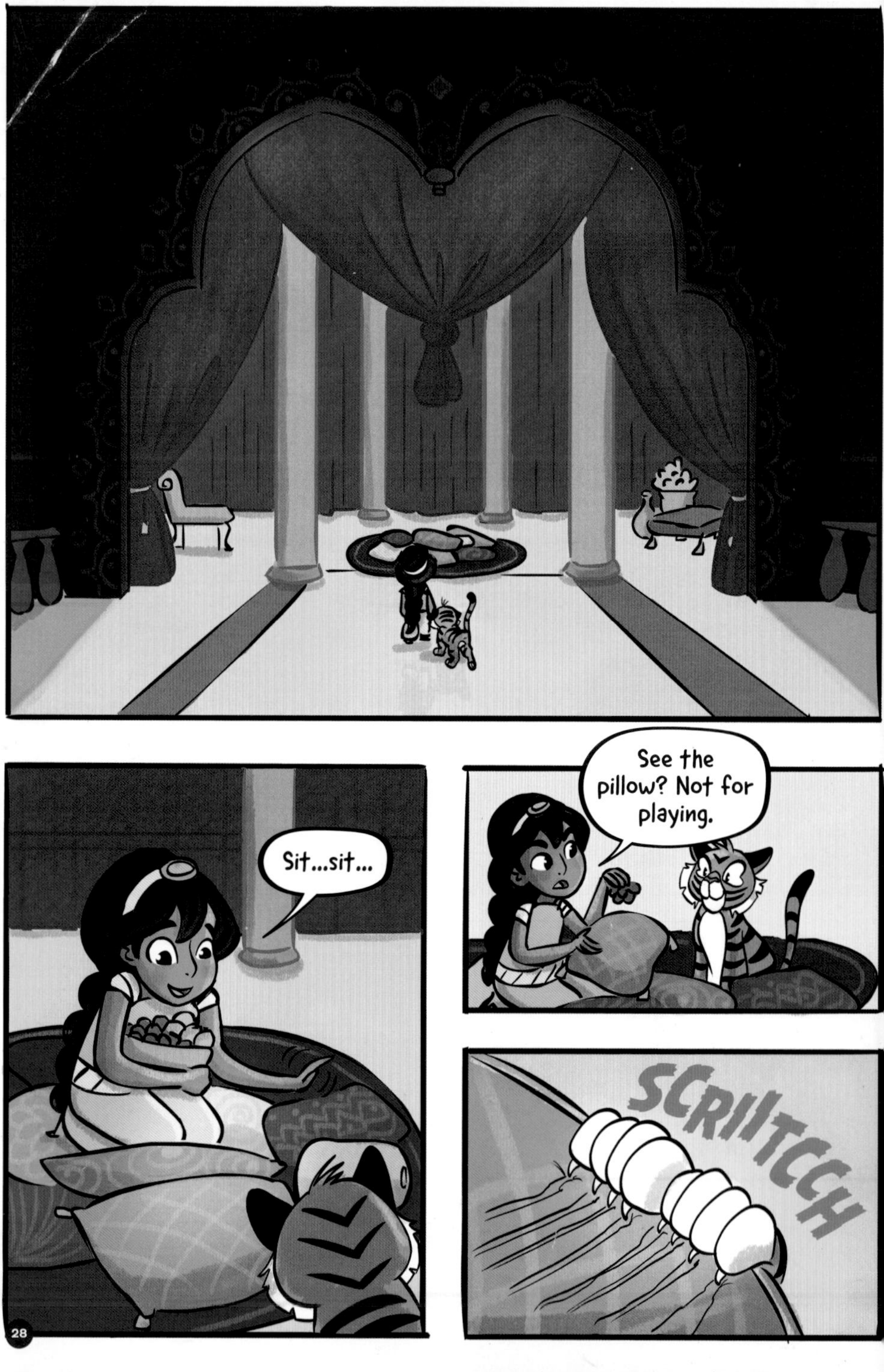
Sit...sit...
See the pillow? Not for playing.
SCRIITCCH

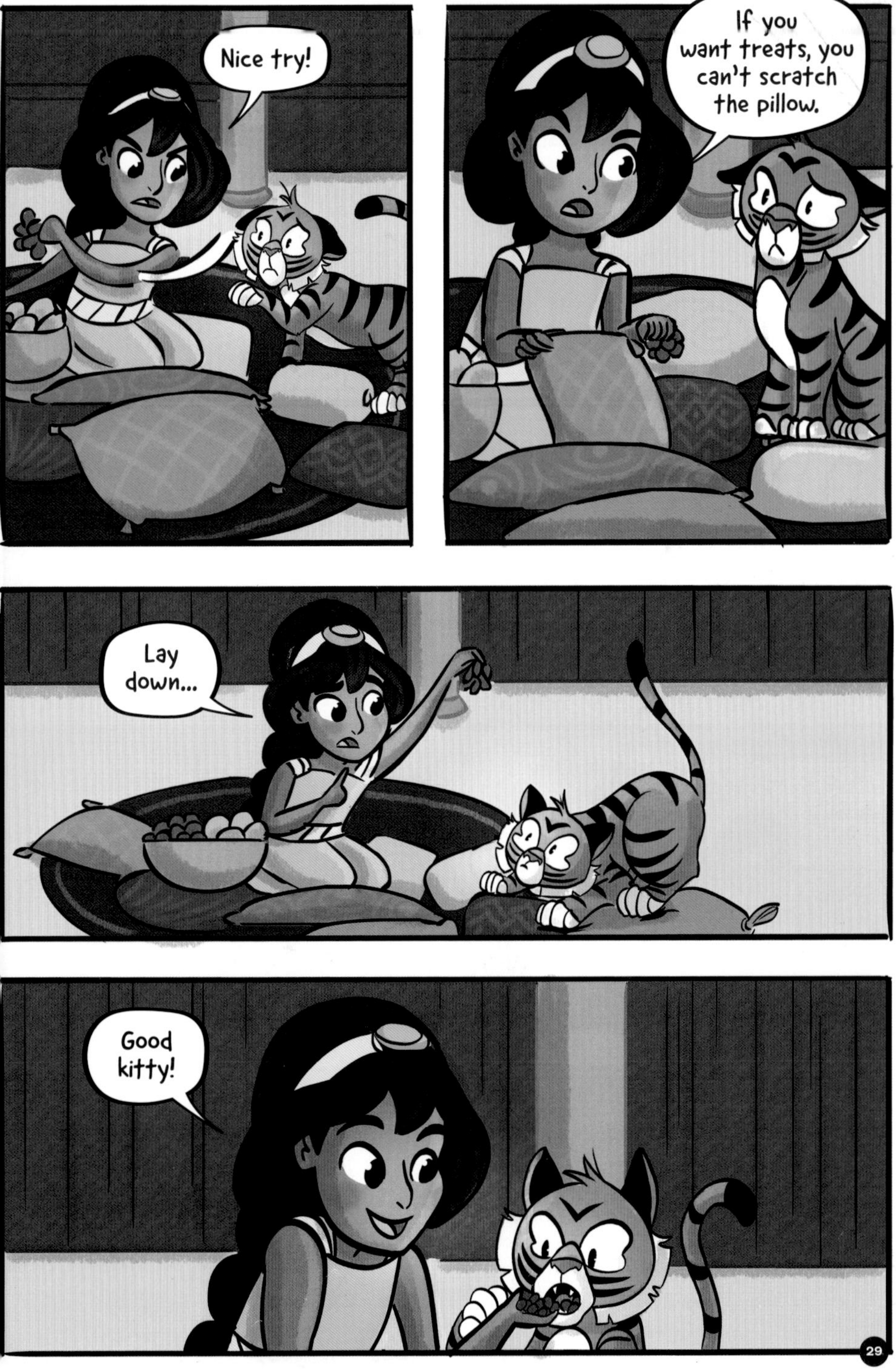
Nice try!
If you want treats, you can't scratch the pillow.
Lay down...
Good kitty!

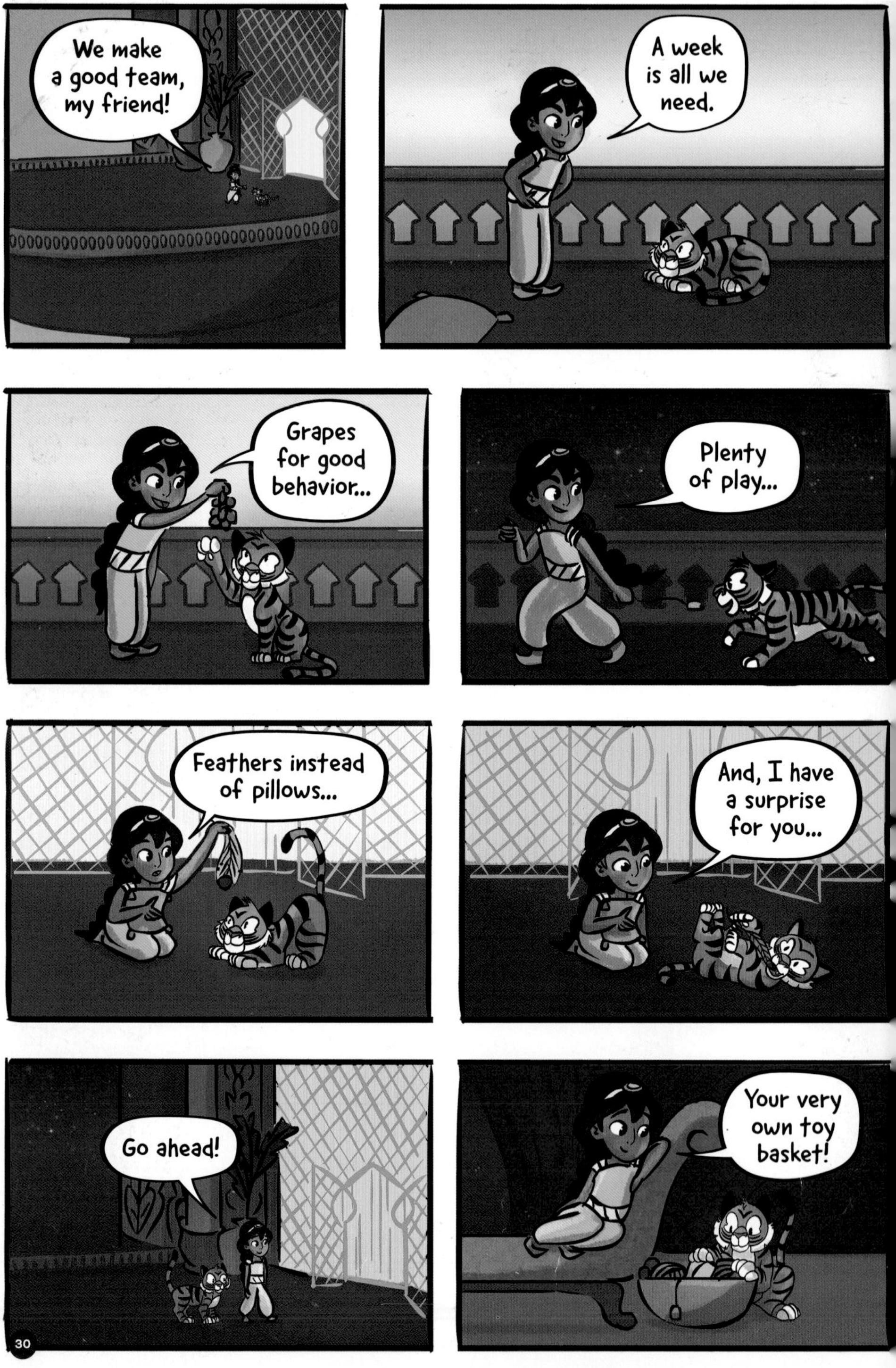
We make a good team, my friend!
A week is all we need.
Grapes for good behavior...
Plenty of play...
Feathers instead of pillows...
And, I have a surprise for you...
Go ahead!
Your very own toy basket!

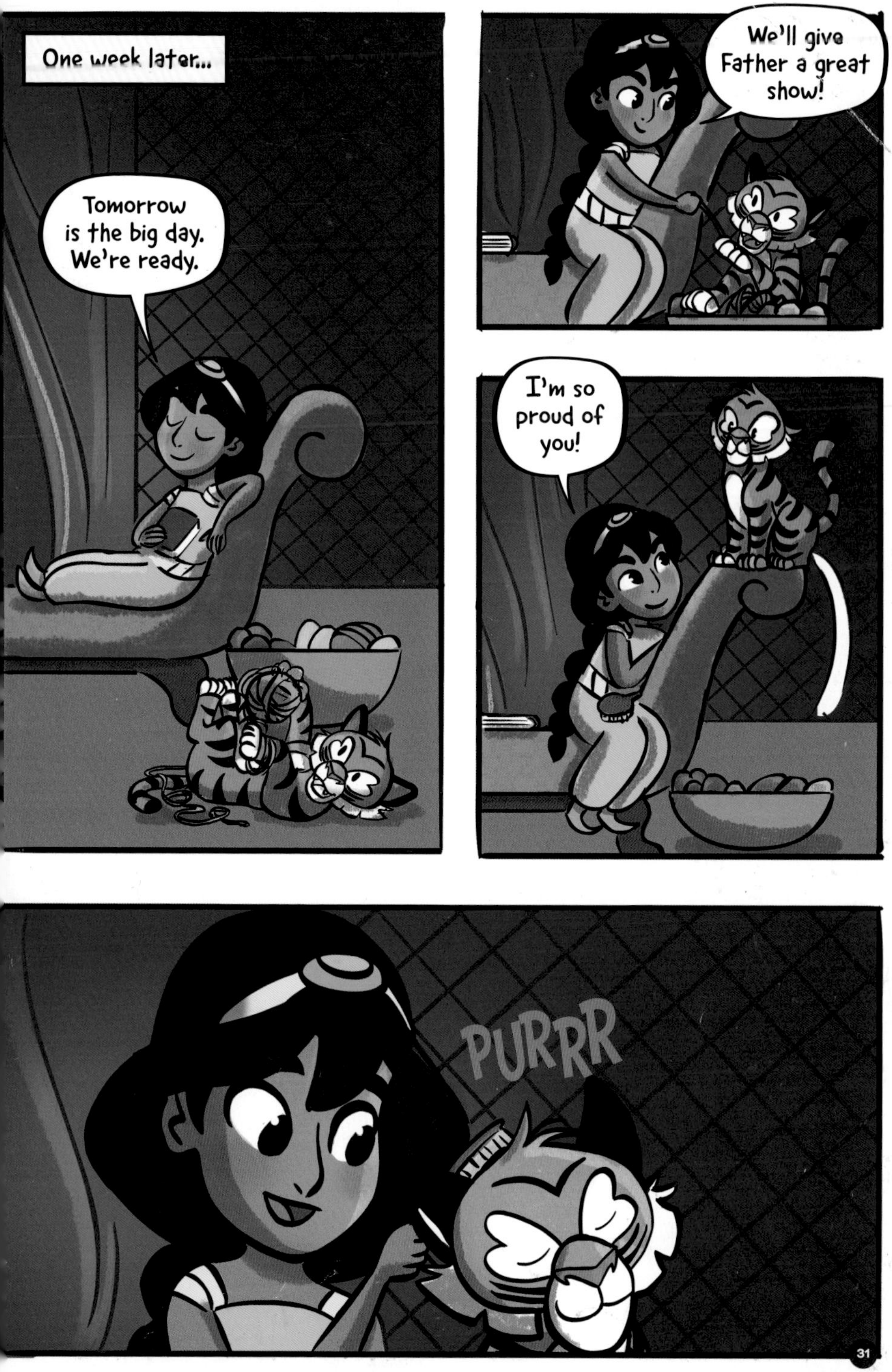
One week later...
Tomorrow is the big day. We're ready.
We'll give Father a great show!
I'm so proud of you!
PURRR

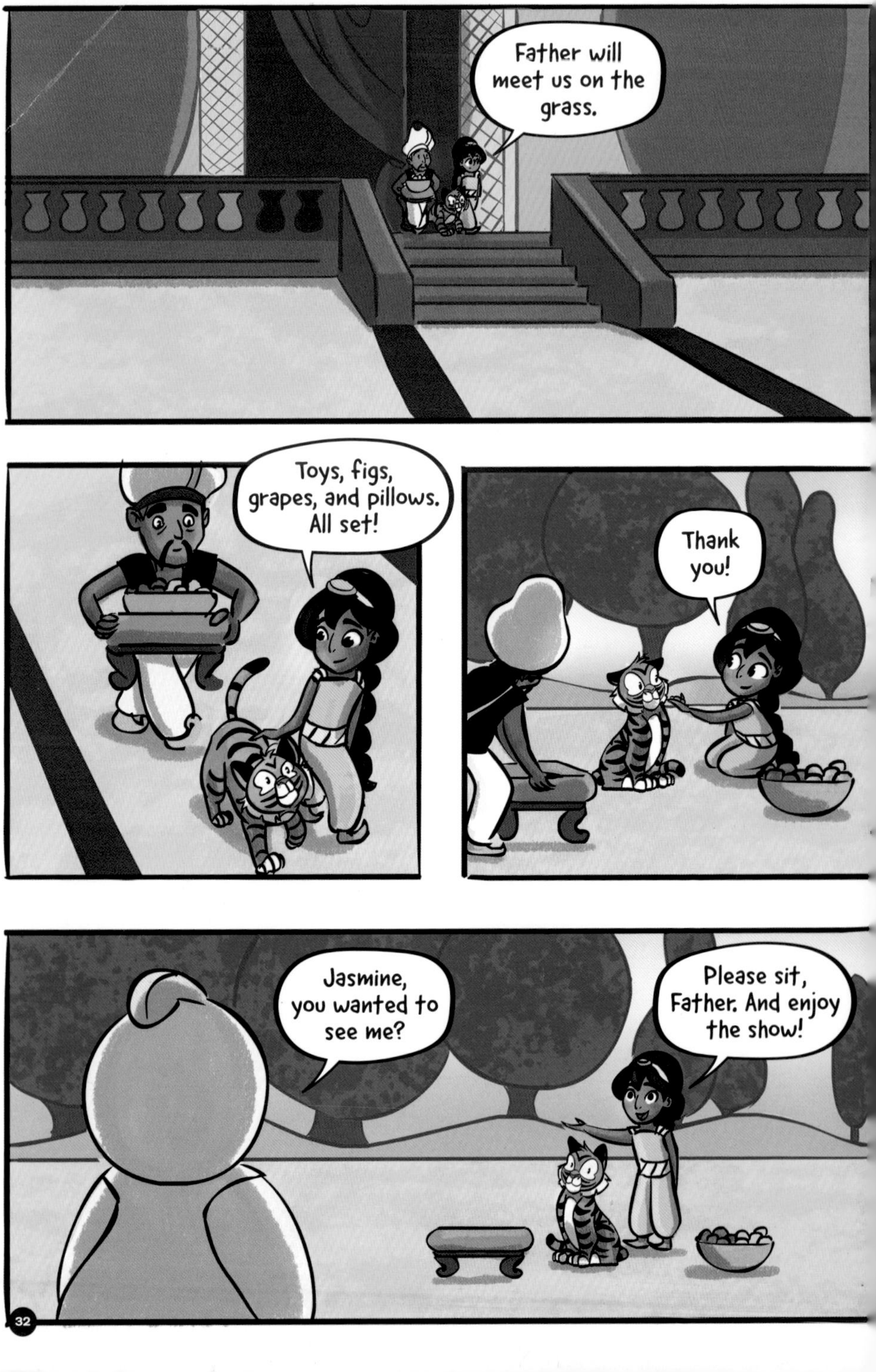
Father will meet us on the grass.
Toys, figs, grapes, and pillows. All set!
Thank you!
Jasmine, you wanted to see me?
Please sit, Father. And enjoy the show!

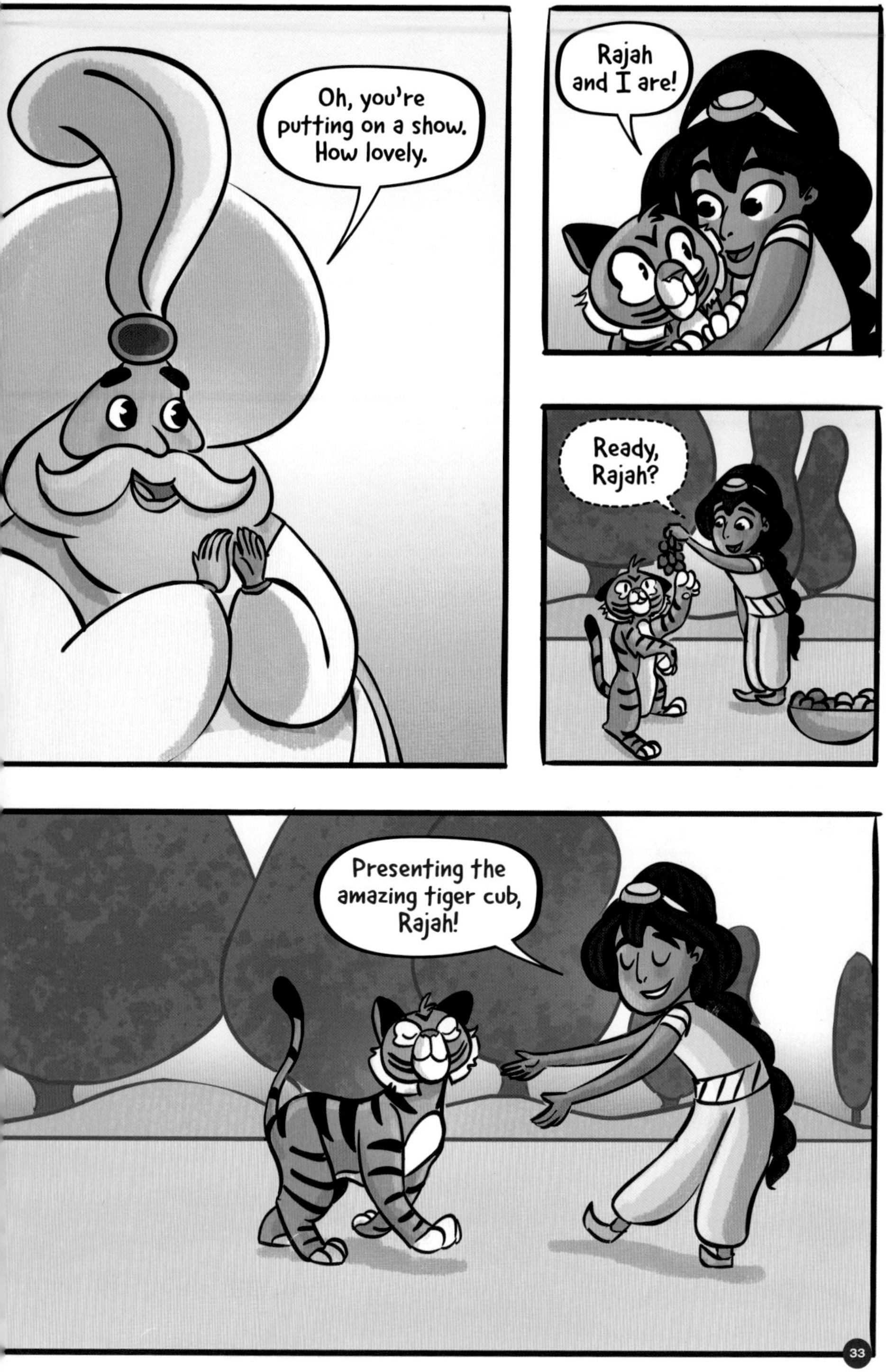
Oh, you're putting on a show. How lovely.
Rajah and I are!
Ready, Rajah?
Presenting the amazing tiger cub, Rajah!

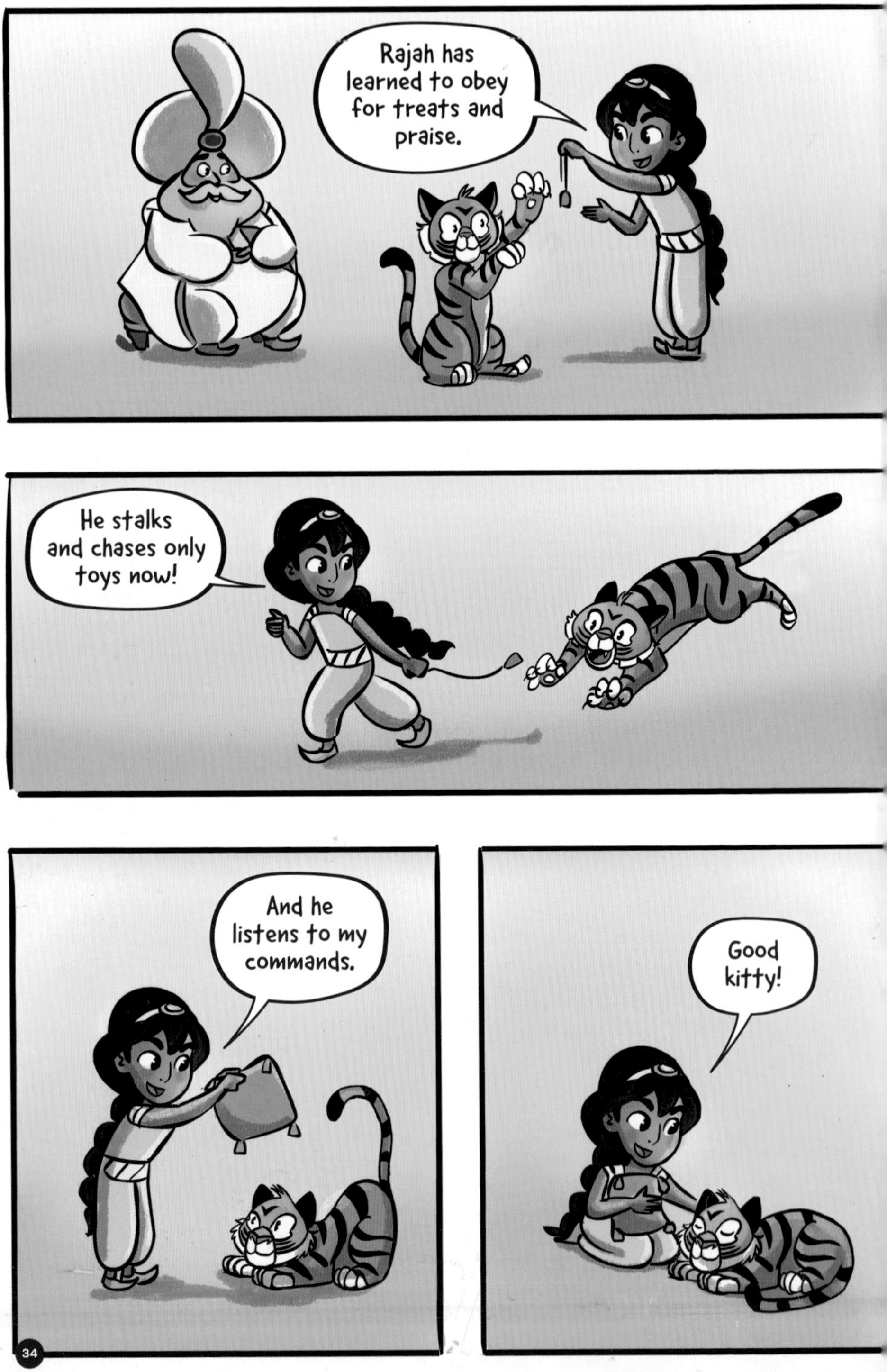
Rajah has learned to obey for treats and praise.
He stalks and chases only toys now!
And he listens to my commands.
Good kitty!

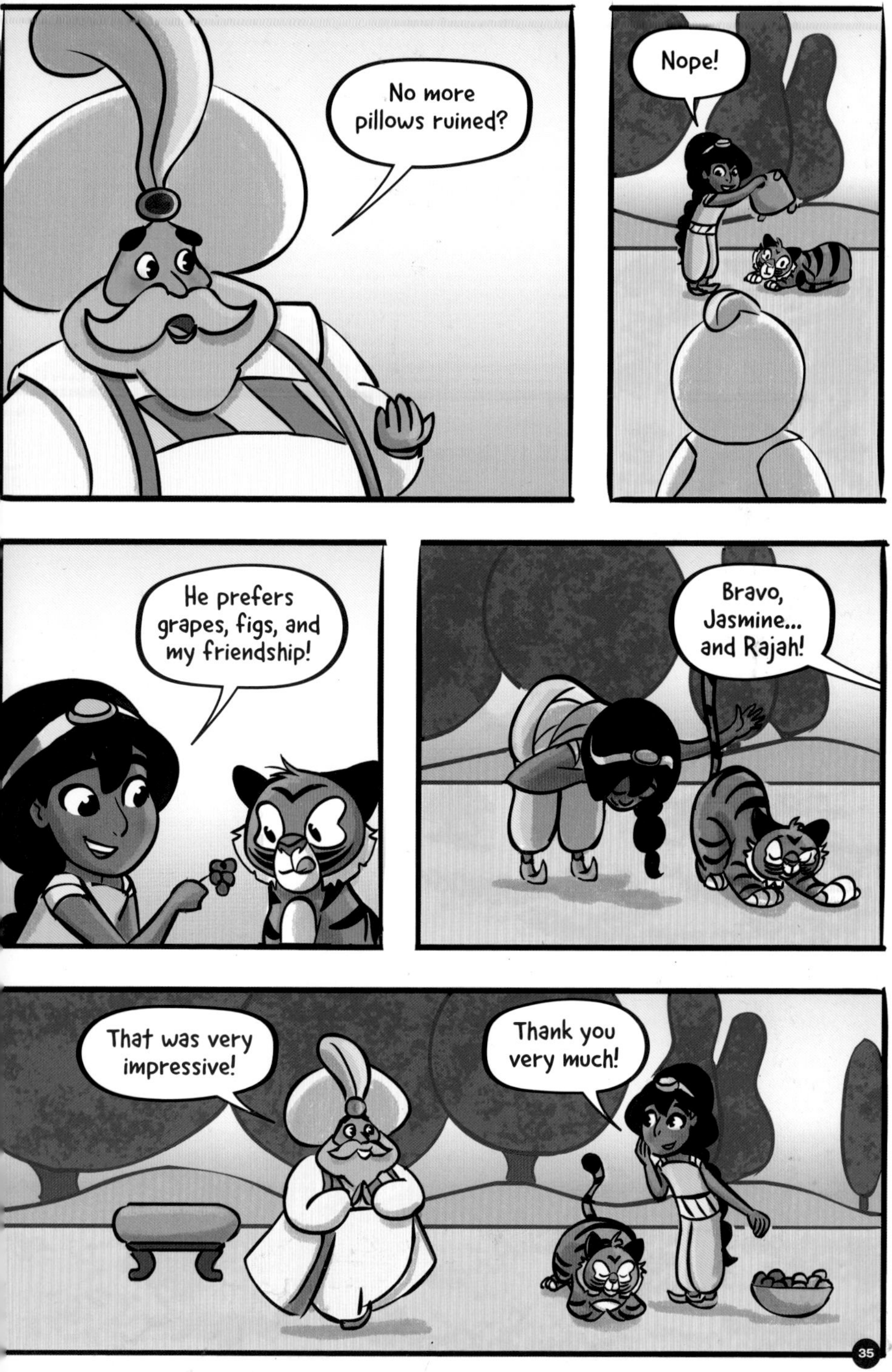
No more pillows ruined?
Nope!
He prefers grapes, figs, and my friendship!
Bravo, Jasmine... and Rajah!
That was very impressive!
Thank you very much!

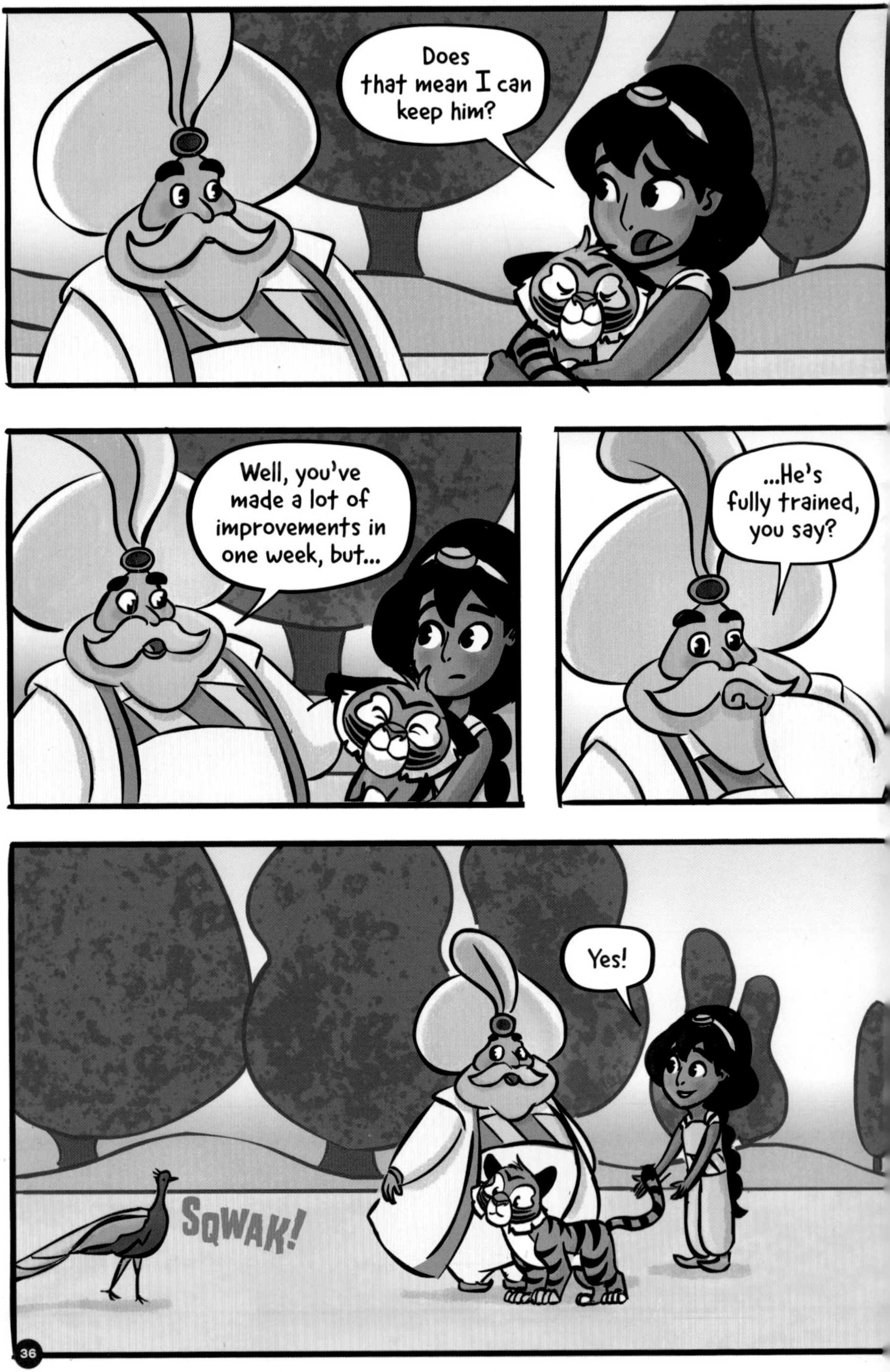
Does that mean I can keep him?
Well, you've made a lot of improvements in one week, but...
...He's fully trained, you say?
Yes!
SQWAK!

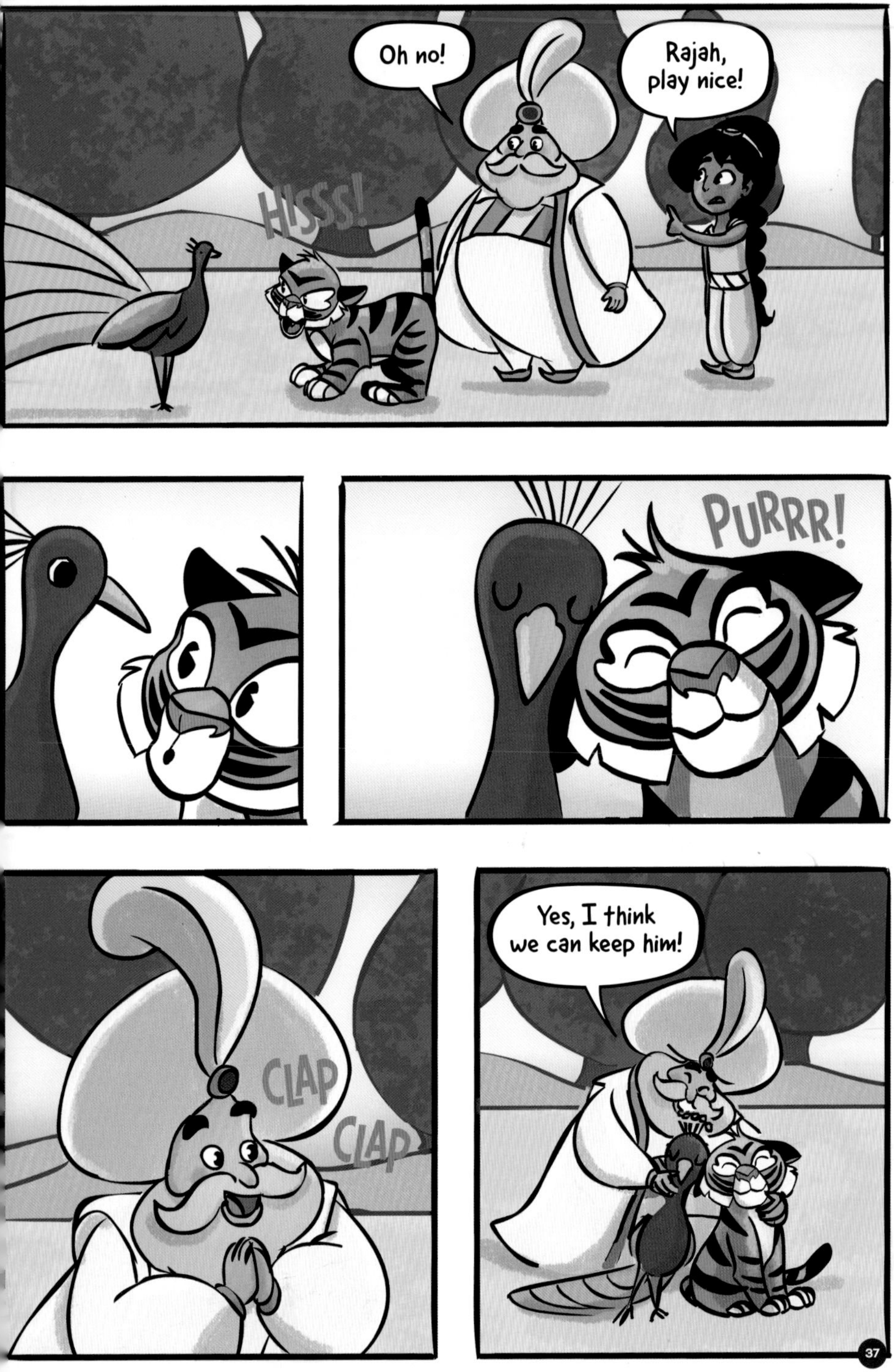
Oh no!
Rajah, play nice!
HISSS!
PURRR!
CLAP
CLAP
Yes, I think we can keep him!

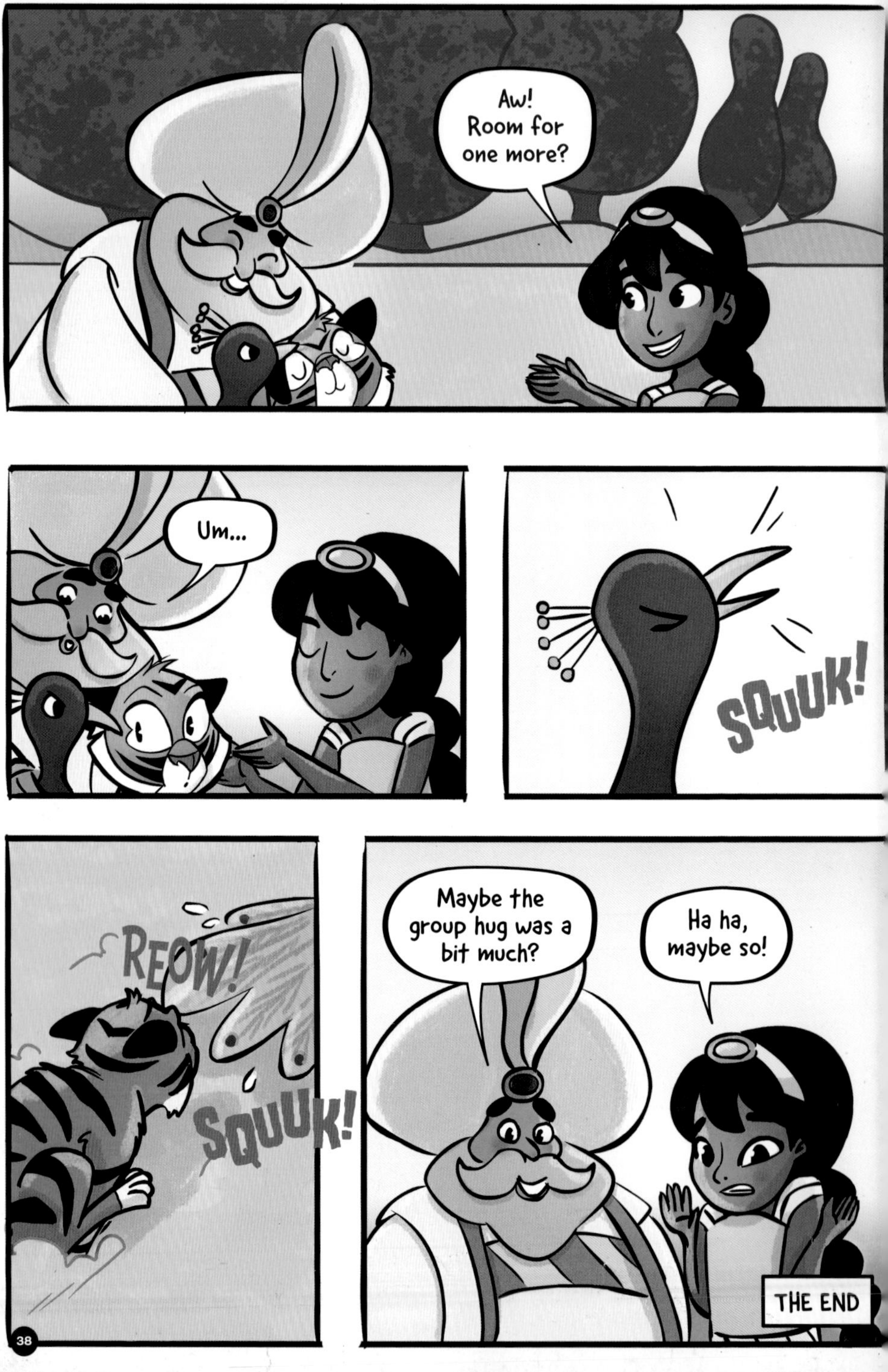
Aw!
Room for
one more?
Um...
SQUUK!
REOW!
SQUUK!
Maybe the group hug was a bit much?
Ha ha, maybe so!
THE END

# Activities to Astound and Amuse You!

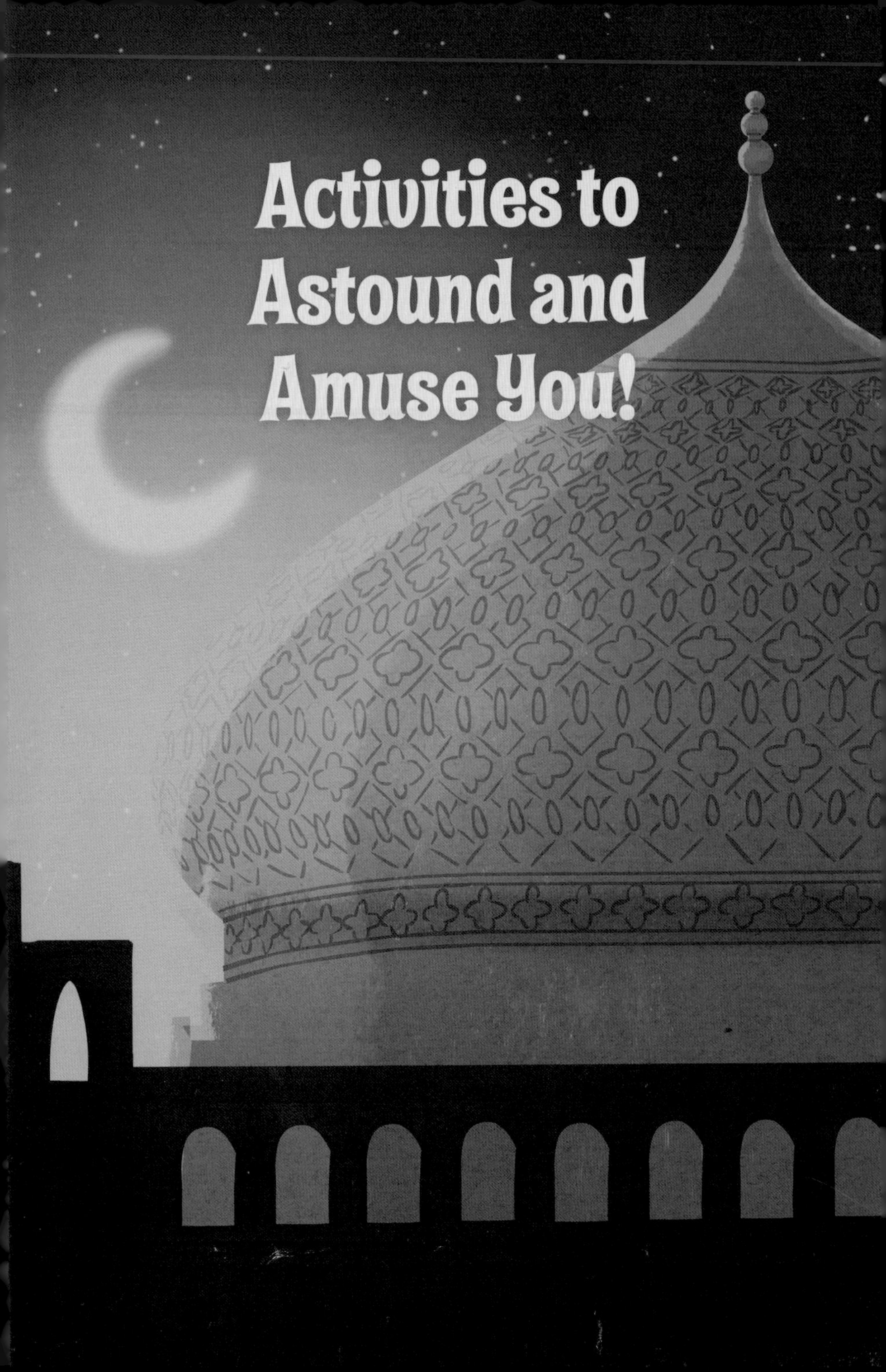

# What Happens Next?

**Think about all the different things that Jasmine and Rajah did in the story you just read.**

Now that Jasmine has trained her tiger Rajah to be well-behaved in the palace, what do you think will happen next?

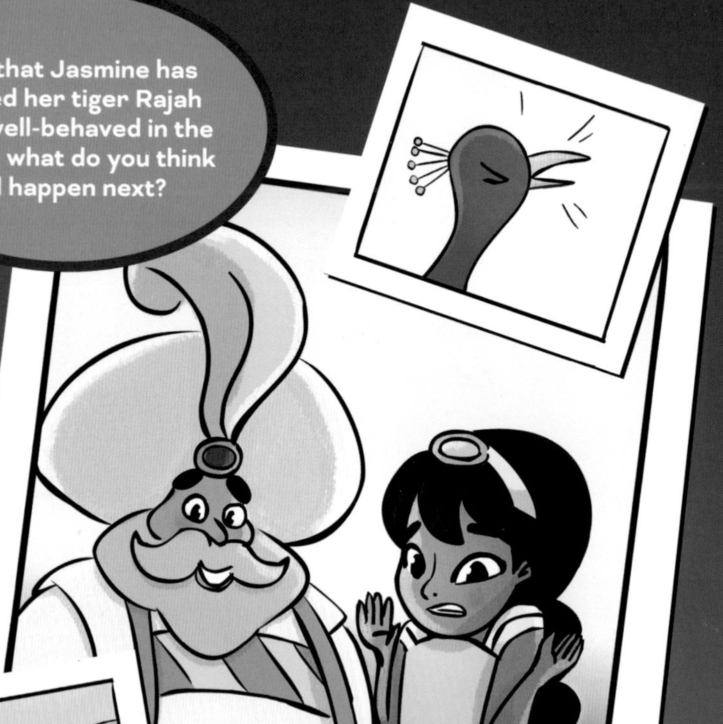

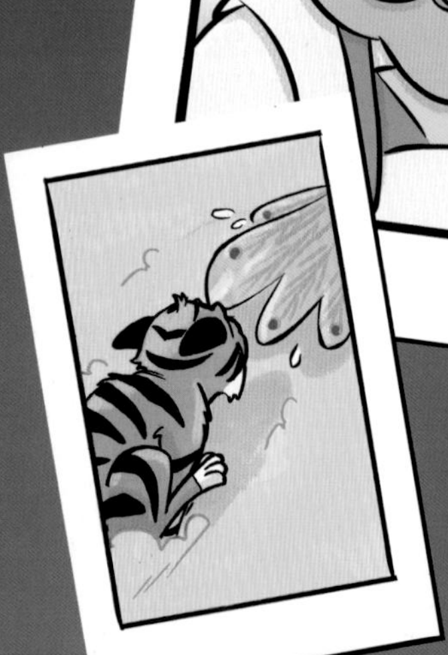

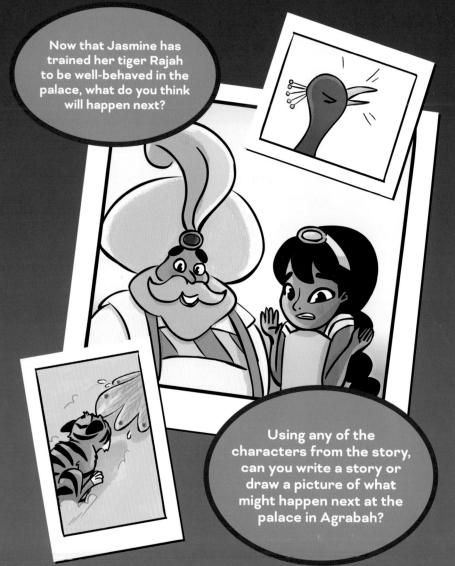

Using any of the characters from the story, can you write a story or draw a picture of what might happen next at the palace in Agrabah?

# What Animal Am I?

**For this activity, you'll need a partner!**

Imagine yourself as an animal. Maybe you're a tiger like Rajah, or maybe you're a peacock, or maybe you're some other kind of animal altogether. Once you've chosen your animal, keep it a secret from your partner! They are going to try to guess what kind of animal you are!

**Tiger**

**Peacock**

Once you've picked your animal, your partner can start asking you questions about yourself, until they can guess what animal you are. But here's the hard part: you can only answer questions with "yes," "no," or "I don't know."

**Below are a few examples of questions your partner might ask you!**
- **Do you have fur?**
- **Do you fly?**
- **Do you have sharp teeth?**
- **Do you live on land?**
- **Do you like to eat fruit?**

When your partner has successfully guessed what you are, swap roles! Have your partner imagine they are a type of animal and *you* ask the questions.

# True or False?

Now that you and Jasmine have learned about the joy of having a cat, can you tell which of these facts about domestic (house) cats are true and which ones are false?

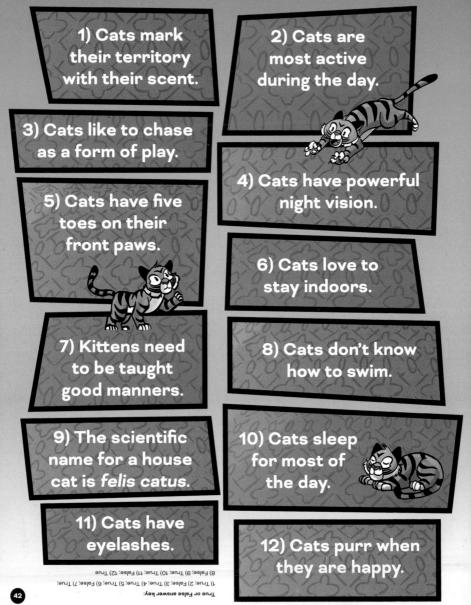

1) Cats mark their territory with their scent.

2) Cats are most active during the day.

3) Cats like to chase as a form of play.

4) Cats have powerful night vision.

5) Cats have five toes on their front paws.

6) Cats love to stay indoors.

7) Kittens need to be taught good manners.

8) Cats don't know how to swim.

9) The scientific name for a house cat is *felis catus*.

10) Cats sleep for most of the day.

11) Cats have eyelashes.

12) Cats purr when they are happy.

True or False answer key:
1) True; 2) False; 3) True; 4) True; 5) True; 6) False; 7) True;
8) False; 9) True; 10) True; 11) True; 12) True

# Scavenger Hunt!

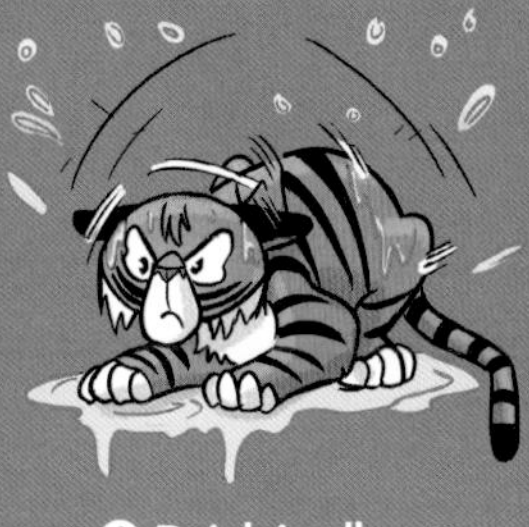

❶ Rajah is all wet

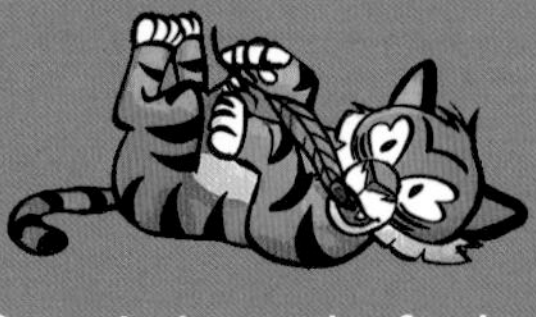

❷ Rajah plays with a feather

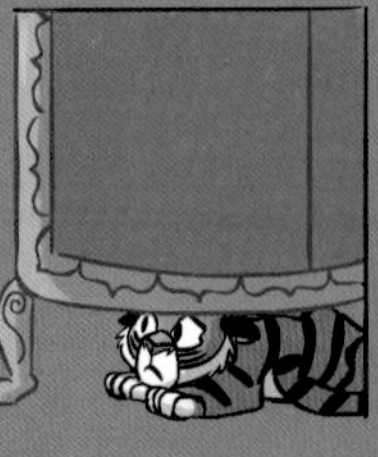

❸ Rajah hides

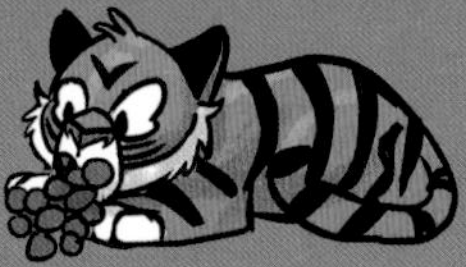

❺ Rajah eats grapes

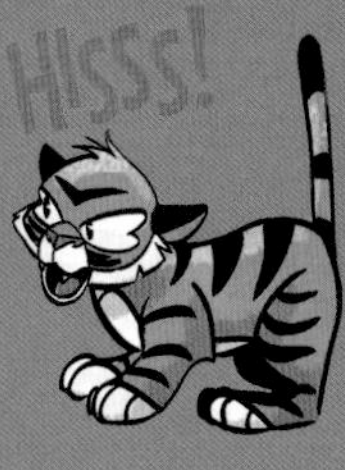
HISSS!

❹ Rajah is hissing

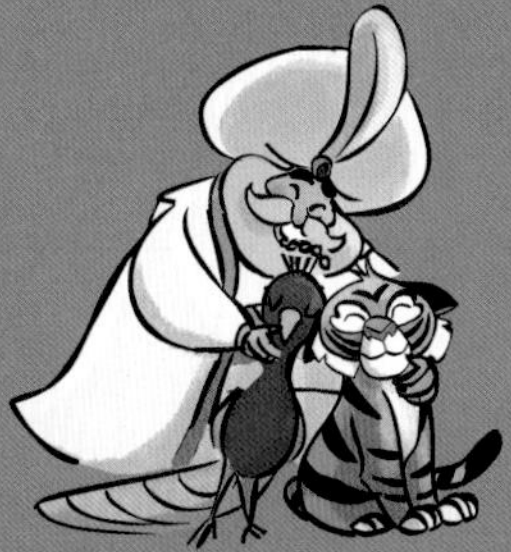

❻ Rajah is hugged by the Sultan

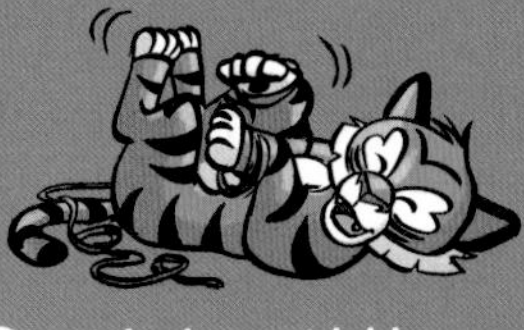

❼ Rajah plays with blue yarn

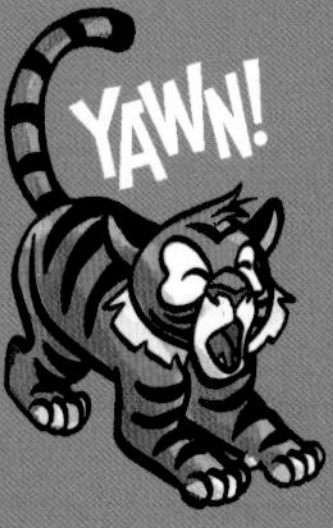
YAWN!

❾ Rajah yawns

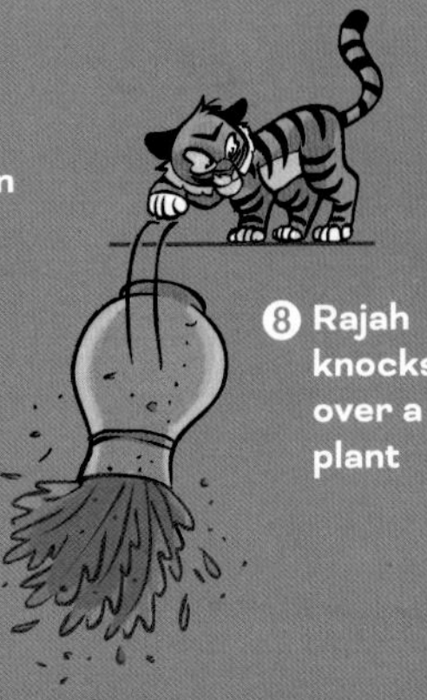

❽ Rajah knocks over a plant

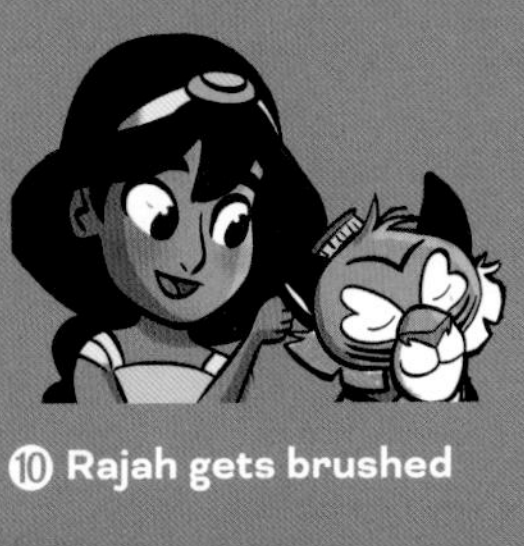

❿ Rajah gets brushed

**Scavenger Hunt answer key:**
1) Rajah is all wet, page 25; 2) Rajah plays with a feather, page 30; 3) Rajah hides, page 8; 4) Rajah is hissing, page 37; 5) Rajah eats grapes, page 26; 6) Rajah is hugged by the Sultan, page 37; 7) Rajah plays with blue yarn, page 12; 8) Rajah knocks over a plant, page 16; 9) Rajah yawns, page 17; 10) Rajah gets brushed, page 31

# Make an Acrostic Poem!

What exactly *is* an acrostic poem? This type of poem uses each of the letters in a topic word to begin each line of a poem. The lines of this poem can be sentences, or phases, or single words—but each line must describe or relate to the topic word.

Now that you know a little about acrostic poems, let's create some! You can try it here (or on a separate piece of paper) using the names of the characters from the story as topic words!

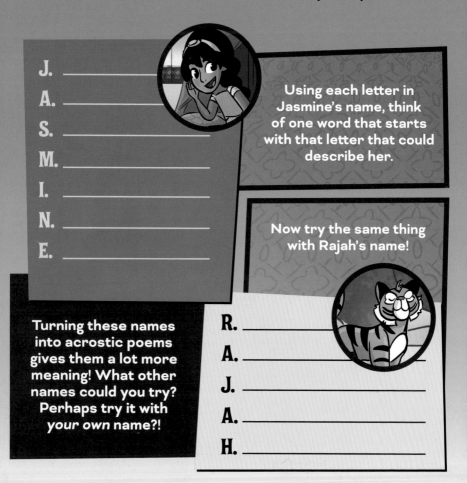

J. _____

A. _____

S. _____

M. _____

I. _____

N. _____

E. _____

Using each letter in Jasmine's name, think of one word that starts with that letter that could describe her.

Now try the same thing with Rajah's name!

Turning these names into acrostic poems gives them a lot more meaning! What other names could you try? Perhaps try it with *your own* name?!

R. _____

A. _____

J. _____

A. _____

H. _____

# Story Recall!

**Do you remember the details of the story that you just read about Princess Jasmine and Rajah? Try your best to answer the questions below from memory. If you can't remember the answers to them all, challenge yourself to read the story again and find the answers!**

1) What time of day is it at the beginning of the story?

2) Why does Rajah need training?

3) How long does the Sultan give Jasmine to train Rajah?

4) How does Jasmine learn what she needs to do to train Rajah?

5) What kind of animal does Rajah chase near the fountain?

6) How does Jasmine find out what kind of fruit Rajah likes to eat?

7) What kind of fruit does Rajah like to eat?

8) What kind of fruit does Rajah *not* like to eat?

9) How does Jasmine show the Sultan that Rajah has been trained?

10) What does the Sultan give Rajah at the end of the story?

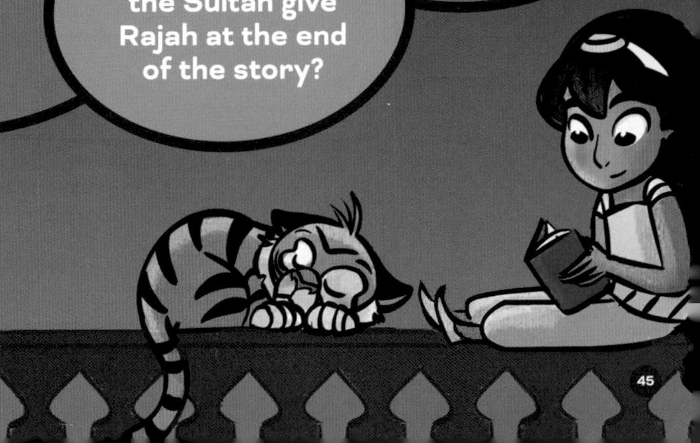

Story Recall answer key:
1) Morning; 2) He scratches and chews things he shouldn't; 3) One week; 4) She reads a book on training cats; 5) A bird; 6) The man with the fruit basket tells her; 7) Grapes and figs; 8) Musk melon; 9) She and Rajah put on a show; 10) A hug

# Fill in the Blank!

**For this activity, you'll need a partner!**

This is a word replacement game! Throughout the short story below, there are blank spaces for you to fill in with different parts of speech. Underneath each blank, there is a listing to tell you what part of speech to use there.

Before you read the story, have your partner go through the story and look for the blanks that need to be filled in. Your partner can ask you for the part of speech that is needed for each blank, and make a list of them, in order. Once you've picked words for all of the blanks, then you—or your partner—can read the story.

Here is a guide to some of the different parts of speech:
*noun:* a person, place, or thing
*adjective:* a word that describes a noun
*verb:* a word that shows an action
*adverb:* a word that describes how you do an action
*interjection:* a short word or phrase that expresses emotion

## Storks in Agrabah

It was a warm evening in the kingdom of Agrabah. Jasmine and Rajah were outside _____**1**_____ the _____**2**_____ air on the _____**3**_____
_____       _____       _____
verb ending in -ing              adjective           noun (a place)

when suddenly a _____**4**_____ flock of storks flew overhead. Jasmine
_____
adjective

said, "_____**5**_____! Rajah, look at the_____**6**_____birds!" Rajah was
_____                                          _____
Interjection                                          adjective

_____**7**_____ to see the flock and _____**8**_____ into the air, ready to play
_____                              _____
adjective                                verb (past tense)

with them. Jasmine _____**9**_____, and she _____**10**_____ behind
                     _____          _____
                     verb (past tense)          verb (past tense)

Rajah's ears, saying, "You would love to have more friendly birds to

_____**11**_____ with here at the palace, wouldn't you?" Just then, the Sultan
_____
verb

entered exclaiming, "_____**12**_____? My _____**13**_____ daughter, a tiger is
                       _____       _____
                       Interjection            adjective

a lot for you to take care of already, we must _____**14**_____ a while before we
                                                _____
                                                verb

get another pet!" Jasmine _____**15**_____ at the Sultan and replied, "Oh,
                           _____
                           verb (past tense)

Father, _____**16**_____! Rajah and I are so _____**17**_____together, I wasn't
         _____                       _____
         interjection                            adjective

thinking of _____**18**_____ any new pets . . . not yet."
             _____
             verb ending in -ing

**DARK HORSE BOOKS**

president and publisher Mike Richardson · collection editor Freddye Miller
collection assistant editors Jenny Blenk, Judy Khuu · collection designer Cindy Cacerez-Sprague
collection activities designer Anita Magaña · digital art technician Christianne Gillenardo-Goudreau

Neil Hankerson Executive Vice President · Tom Weddle Chief Financial Officer · Randy Stradley Vice President
of Publishing · Nick McWhorter Chief Business Development Officer · Matt Parkinson Vice President of
Marketing · Dale LaFountain Vice President of Information Technology · Cara Niece Vice President of
Production and Scheduling · Mark Bernardi Vice President of Book Trade and Digital Sales · Ken Lizzi General
Counsel · Dave Marshall Editor in Chief · Davey Estrada Editorial Director · Chris Warner Senior Books Editor
· Cary Grazzini Director of Specialty Projects · Lia Ribacchi Art Director · Vanessa Todd-Holmes Director of
Print Purchasing · Matt Dryer Director of Digital Art and Prepress · Michael Gombos Director of International
Publishing and Licensing · Kari Yadro Director of Custom Programs

**DISNEY PUBLISHING WORLDWIDE GLOBAL MAGAZINES, COMICS AND PARTWORKS**

Publisher Lynn Waggoner · EDITORIAL TEAM Bianca Coletti (Director, Magazines), Guido Frazzini (Director,
Comics), Carlotta Quattrocolo (Executive Editor), Stefano Ambrosio (Executive Editor, New IP), Camilla Vedove
(Senior Manager, Editorial Development), Behnoosh Khalili (Senior Editor), Julie Dorris (Senior Editor), Mina
Riazi (Assistant Editor), Jonathan Manning (Assistant Editor) · DESIGN Enrico Soave (Senior Designer) · ART
Ken Shue (VP, Global Art), Manny Mederos (Senior Illustration Manager, Comics and Magazines), Roberto
Santillo (Creative Director), Marco Ghiglione (Creative Manager), Stefano Attardi (Computer Art Designer)
· PORTFOLIO MANAGEMENT Olivia Ciancarelli (Director) · BUSINESS & MARKETING Mariantonietta Galla
(Marketing Manager), Virpi Korhonen (Editorial Manager)

**Disney Princess: Jasmine's New Pet**

Published by Dark Horse Books
A division of Dark Horse Comics, Inc.
10956 SE Main Street
Milwaukie, OR 97222

DarkHorse.com

To find a comics shop in your area, visit comicshoplocator.com

First edition: October 2018
ISBN 978-1-50671-052-5
Digital ISBN 978-1-50671-059-4

1 3 5 7 9 10 8 6 4 2
Printed in China

# LOOKING FOR BOOKS FOR YOUNGER READERS?

EACH VOLUME INCLUDES A SECTION OF FUN ACTIVITIES!

$7.99 each!

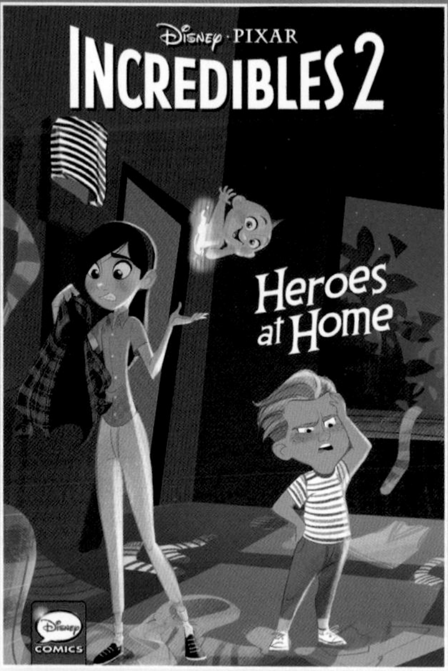

DISNEY · PIXAR
INCREDIBLES 2
Heroes at Home
DISNEY COMICS


**DISNEY•PIXAR INCREDIBLES 2: HEROES AT HOME**

While their mom and dad—Mr. Incredible and Elastigirl—are both taking on new and very different jobs, Dash and Violet are doing their best to help out! First, Dash and Violet go into secret Super mode when they interrupt criminal activity on a routine grocery trip to pick up some essentials! Then, helping out at home, their efforts to keep up on their chores are unknowingly obstructed by the innocent mischief of their little brother, Jack-Jack!

ISBN 978-1-50670-943-7 | $7.99

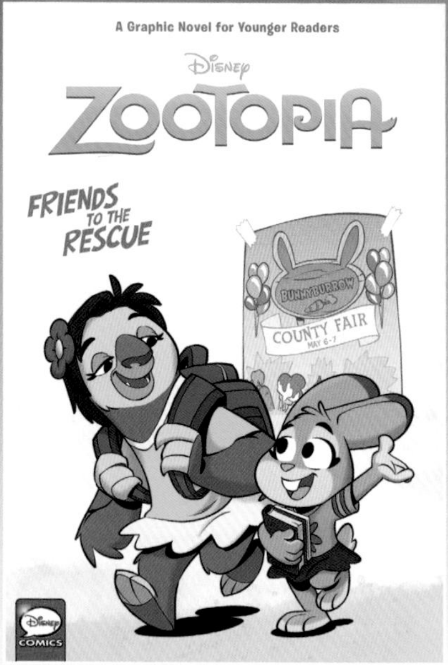

A Graphic Novel for Younger Readers
DISNEY
ZOOTOPIA
FRIENDS TO THE RESCUE
BUNNYBURROW
COUNTY FAIR
MAY 6-7
DISNEY COMICS


**DISNEY ZOOTOPIA: FRIENDS TO THE RESCUE**

Judy Hopps is excited for the fun at the Bunnyburrow County Fair, but her friend Dinah has to sneak out of the house to join her! When Dinah stumbles into trouble, it takes both Judy and Dinah's talents to ensure that they both make it safely home. Meanwhile, at his friend Hedy's birthday party, Nick Wilde learns it's the thought that counts. While he might not have enough money to buy a gift, Nick has other talents that he puts to good use for a truly unforgettable celebration.

ISBN 978-1-50671-054-9 | $7.99

**AVAILABLE AT YOUR LOCAL COMICS SHOP OR BOOKSTORE!**
**TO FIND A COMICS SHOP IN YOUR AREA, VISIT COMICSHOPLOCATOR.COM**

For more information or to order direct: On the web: DarkHorse.com
Email: mailorder@darkhorse.com | Phone: 1-800-862-0052 Mon.–Fri. 9 AM to 5 PM Pacific Time